All the Cities of Gold

Karen K. Newell

Learn For Your Life Publishing
Camp Hill, PA 17011

Cover Design by Christy Short
About the cover: The photo depicts Donna's granddaughter, Krista,as
the model holding Donna's doll which was later restored by Hazel.
Photograph by Emily Wells. The pattern of the family tapestry can
be seen faded in the background on the front cover. Photograph by
Christy Short.

Literary license was used to reconstruct dialogue and the events
recorded in the book. Only a few minor characters are fictitious,
including the names of some classmates and Jimmy and Sarah in the
transient camp. All other characters and major events are real.

ISBN 9781508501619

www.Learn4YourLife.com

All the Cities of Gold

Give Me A Home

Oh give me a home where the buffalo roam,
Where the deer and the antelope play,
Where seldom is heard a discouraging word,
And the skies are not cloudy all day.

Where the air is so pure, and the breezes so free,
The colors so vivid and bold,
That I would not exchange my home on the range,
For all of the cities of gold.

Adapted from the Kansas State Song

Prologue

Give Me A Home

Prologue

Train to Kansas

1948

"I wonder if he even has a home?"

The dark brown eyes of a fourteen year old girl focused on the man in army fatigues sitting two rows in front of her on the opposite side of the train. As the shrieking whistle and screeching brakes announced they were approaching the next station, he leaned forward, face alert, clutching his duffle bag. He appeared to be the only passenger getting off at this stop.

The girl's eyes narrowed as she surveyed him as if she was thinking of something. Like herself, the man was traveling alone. Perhaps he also wondered who, if anyone, would be waiting for him.

She turned and stared out her window with disinterest as the train slowed. Trains made frequent stops to these small towns dotted across the Midwest. Rounding the last corner, she detected a crowd gathered on the station platform. Her eyes widened and she glanced again at the soldier. From where he sat, he could not see them yet. Her head and shoulders rose in interest. She watched as people standing on the crowded platform pointed excitedly toward their approaching train.

The soldier grasped his duffle bag and made his way to the train's exit. As he emerged onto the platform the crowd erupted with cheers. Those on-board watched as one woman, surely his mother, broke from the crowd to embrace him – crying unashamedly. Neighbors and friends crowded around. Even a frantic collie barked an ecstatic welcome.

The girl on-board the train heard a small gasp from the

elderly woman next to her. She glanced over and saw that she too was watching as America's countryside welcomed one more soldier home. Over the last three years they had returned one by one: soldiers and sailors and marines.

Witnesses on-board the train wiped silent tears, many re-membering similar reunions with their own loved ones. Some were reminded once more of those who would not return.

The thin, sandy-haired girl at the window watched, dry eyed. Her tears had stopped long ago. The scene outside in the bright summer day brought back bitter-sweet memories of the day her father had returned from the Great War in Europe. "Was it only three years ago?" she wondered.

***

"Donna! Donna! It's for you!"

Donna steered the orange Allis Chalmers tractor through the field. Her aunt's voice rose above the sound of the engine. She turned her head toward the voice.

Aunt Cora was hurrying down the steps of the farmhouse, across the yard, waving her apron. Donna raised her eye brows, surprised to see her gentle and proper aunt wildly beckoning her to come. She turned off the tractor and slid off.

"It's for you, Donna," Aunt Cora gasped breathlessly. "Your father! He's on the phone!"

Without waiting, Donna bolted toward the porch of their farmhouse. Up two stairs, into the kitchen; she barely stopped even when the dimness of the house blinded her eyes accustomed to the bright sunshine.

An old fashioned crank phone was on the wall. She snatched the receiver lying on the end table. "Hello!" she yelled into the telephone.

"That you, Donna?" his cheerful drawl crackled from the other end of the line.

"Daddy! Daddy! Is that you? Are you back from Germany?"

"Yup, safe and sound." It was the unmistakable sound of her father's voice. "Just got off the ship and back on American soil a few minutes ago."

"When will I see you?"

"Soon, I hope. Very soon."

It was a quick conversation. Phone calls were expensive, but it was worth every dime to hear his voice.

She threw her arms around Aunt Cora, now standing at her side breathlessly. They were both laughing and crying. "He's home. He's home. He's really, really coming home."

***

Back on the train, Donna sighed. She had wept with happiness at her father's return on that day so long ago. It was the last time she had cried – until a few weeks ago.

"Things didn't turn out as I expected," she reminisced. "I guess they never do."

It was a bit hard to figure out just what she had expected anyway. That she and her brothers would live at home together with their mother and father. After all, isn't that the way it's supposed to work?

Then no one would ever whisper behind her back again.

She remembered the first time it happened. Kids were playing tag in the front yard of their one room, country school house when she arrived before the first bell. Happily, Donna joined in as she always had. Abruptly, the game stopped.

"Who said you could play?" demanded Alex Owens.

"Of course Donna can play too," said Maxine.

"No she can't," retorted Alex's sister, Janet with both hands on her hips. "My mother says we aren't allowed to play with *her.*"

"Why?" asked little Donna, stung by the rejection.

"Because," replied Janet, "her parents are getting divorced."

"What's 'divorced'?" asked one of the second grade girls.

Donna wanted to know too. She wasn't privy to the explanation that Janet whispered to the small knot of children gathered around her.

"What does 'divorce' mean?" Donna asked her grandmother when she got home from school that afternoon. Instead of an explanation, Donna was given additional chores.

There was always another reason she wasn't living with her parents. Her father was working in the next town. She and her older brother were staying at their grandparents' farm for the summer. She was visiting Aunt Cora and Uncle Nathan.

But eventually everyone knew.

Donna fell asleep in their truck one day and when she woke up she heard her father telling her older brother that he was not going to be married to their mother any more. Their mother never said any thing to them. Soon, her parents' divorce was official. She and her two brothers were sent to different relatives and moved from place to place. Then her father went to Germany and the war.

She had worried about him. Scenes from the war front blazed across the screen before the Saturday matinee; the pleasure of the movie dimmed as she watched the footage of actual battles and remembered her father was over there. "Dad will come home," she had told herself. "Then everything will go back to normal again."

He came back. But he did not come home. Not to Kansas .

Her father moved to Massachusetts and married Marion, her stepmother. They wanted Donna to come live with them. She had felt grown up flying on the commercial airplane to Massachusetts by herself. Leaving Kansas, she had also left her mother and brothers, grandparents, aunts, uncles and security behind.

Now here she was sitting on the train heading back to Kansas.

As the train slowly pulled away from the platform, the picture of the soldier surrounded by a gleeful crowd disappeared behind her right shoulder. A gas station and small grocery store came into view and then disappeared also. Now she was staring at one of the many wheat fields growing across the Midwest.

The train gathered speed as Donna and the other passengers were jostled in their seats. They heard the whistle blare its fierce warning to the outside world to keep off the tracks. The wheels against the tracks made a rhythmic sound.

"Divorced. Unwanted. Divorced. Unwanted," the rails seemed to chant.

Donna looked down at her feet. Her stylish shoes and matching purse were a contrast to the faded carpet of the coach.

Kithy had helped her pick them out. Kithy was her stepmother's mother. She had watched Donna with humor as she had gone to store after store, carefully choosing things she would wear to Kansas. It was Kithy who had snacks ready for her when she came home from her large suburban school. Then when Marion came home from the elementary school where she taught, the two women would listen to Donna recount the activities of her day.

How different her school was from the country school house she had gone to in Kansas. So many kids and different teachers, it was a contrast to the small but well-ordered rural

13

school that provided the first years of her education.   Saturday nights kids from her class came to the square dances her father held. Sometimes on the weekends she and Marion and Kithy would go to Boston.

"Are you going home?" the voice of the woman next to her broke into Donna's thoughts.

"I, I'm going to Kansas," Donna stuttered trying to find the right words to answer the simple question. "To see my mother," she finished lamely.

The woman looked at her quizzically, then nodded in understanding. "You have a long trip," she commented before returning to her magazine.

Donna looked down at her purse. She could imagine the pictures she carried in it without even opening it.   Her brothers. Her father and stepmother's wedding picture.   And her mother's picture.

She had kept her mother's picture in a small frame near her bed. Once, she had left it on the bedside table and Marion had seen it. Her stepmother had been angry with Donna for displaying the picture of her mother. Marion was quiet and unresponsive whenever Donna mentioned her mother at all. So Donna never talked about her. But she kept her mother's picture hidden in her dresser drawer.   And now she had that picture in her purse. Maybe, she hoped, she could find why her mother was not a proper subject for conversation when she got home.

"Home," muttered Donna to herself. "Am I leaving home or going home?" she wondered.

Her finger twirled around her light brown hair and she frowned out the window.   What made it all so complicated? Would Marion and Kithy ever forgive her when they found out she wanted to stay in Kansas to live with her mother? The same

14

mother whose name brought cold stares when it was uttered? Would she then be allowed to visit them in Massachusetts the way they were sending her to visit her Kansas relatives now?

Suddenly a thought occurred to Donna. Would people come to welcome her as they did for the soldier? Would her aunts and uncles still be interested in her? Another nagging question was even too difficult to put into words. "Will Mother even be there?"

Or had they all forgotten her, moving on with their own lives once she had left? Was she simply returning to a memory, like an old faded photograph?

The countryside darted passed her window. Donna rested her head as the rhythmic sway and clatter of the old train made her drowsy. Fields, woods, old farm houses and small stores blurred. As her heavy eyelids shut, the images outside became a mist of distant scenes from a distant past. She fell asleep and dreamed of people far off.

Part 1

Where the Buffalo Roam

Dodge City

1909

A young woman stuck her head out of the small shack and searched the area before emerging. The last rays of the setting sun swept the rows of the shanty town where she lived.

About twenty poorly constructed buildings made up the camp. They were built out of old wooden crates, scraps of metal, even old tires. A few additional tents were scattered hodge-podge along the outskirts. She had overheard one old-timer bragging that his tent dated all the way from the Civil War.

Right now, she didn't want to talk to or see anyone. Her goal was simply to get to the water pump before the sun would set leaving the camp in a dense darkness. She would have no light to see with when night-time came. Nonetheless she always waited until the end of day when fewer people were about. Now was her chance.

She glanced one last time to make sure the baby was asleep, then scanned the rows up and down to verify no one was around. Swiftly but quietly she picked her way toward the single water pump on the outside of the camp. She carried an old metal pail which would transport the water for her and the baby for the next twenty-four hours.

An old out-house was near the water pump. She put down her pail and made a quick stop at the out-house. Then, picking up the pail again, she headed toward the pump.

Up, down, up, down; it took effort to get the thin trickle

of water to fill her pail. Several times her eyes darted around to make sure no one else was approaching.

"I'm an outcast in a city of outcasts," the young woman muttered dejectedly to herself.

Her name was Florence, though no-one at the camp seemed to know it. She had arrived three months earlier in the first weeks of spring. Late one evening she had trudged into camp, weary and sore. Other women had looked at her growing body, drawn their own conclusions, and turned away from her with derision.

She had come to this camp in Dodge City because she had no other place to go – like all the others here. Bad times, hard luck, wrong choices – the stories were all different, but the outcome was the same.

Not everyone was bad to her. One older woman named Sarah had told her about the shack she now occupied.

"It's a good 'un, you had better take that shack while it's still empty," she had confided to Florence. "Last man in 'der died over the winter. Pneumonia or tuberculosis or somethin'. Used to hear 'im coughin' day after day. Then one day we dint see 'im and we dint hear 'im. Someun checked on 'im and sure 'nuf he was as dead as an old dead fly.

"No one wanted his old shack cuz they was afeard of the germs," Sarah had explained. "But hims been dead awhile now and those germs would have froze up in the last frost we had. It's a good shack, it is. Got a window and a door and a little chimney so's you can light a fire. If you don't take it I'll wager someone else'll be trampin' into camp in a day or so and claim it right quick."

So Florence had moved into the dead man's shack. There was an old cot for her. Her winter coat was used as a blanket when she needed it. Newspapers were spread on the cot to make it more comfortable.

Then the baby had come. She had walked back and forth in her shack as the pains got closer together. Close to the end she had cried out for her mother. But her mother was not here.

But old Sarah had heard her cry out and knew what to do. She had wobbled several blocks to get Dr. Bronson, the only doctor in Dodge City. But by the time he had got to the camp, the baby was already born.

"She's pretty small," was all he said about the little creature Florence held in her arms. Satisfied that he had done all that was needed, he had left. Sarah stayed. She brought Florence some thin soup and dry bread from the charity kitchen the next day.

But now, Sarah was gone. A hobo stopping in for the night had reported there was a household in need of a laundress in a town ten miles north. Sarah packed up the few items she owned and headed north. It was how the transient camps got the name. People with nowhere to go came; and when they found someplace else to go, they went.

"And maybe," thought Florence, "a letter will come tomorrow and I can go back home." Furtively, she made her way from the water pump back to her own shanty. As she approached, she noted it was quiet. The baby was still asleep. She started to open the creaky door when a scraping sound was heard.

As she turned, she saw one of the old-timers approaching with a limp. Part of a foot was missing, and he drug his leg behind him as he walked with a crutch.

"Scuze me, Miss," he called to her. "Not quite as young as I used to be. Mind if I sit a spell at yer door."

Without waiting for an answer, he lowered himself on an old crate sitting outside her hut.

"Whoa, now. It's a hot one," he stated, taking off his tat-

21

tered cowboy hat and wiping his brow. "Hain't been this hot since the summer right before the blizzard of '86."

"You do know about the blizzard of '86, I suppose?" he questioned her.

Florence shook her head to indicate she did not.

"Well, let me tell you 'bout it. Twas 25 years ago, and Dodge City has never been the same. Matter o' fact, not me or many others has been the same."

"What happened?" Florence asked, growing slightly interested in spite of herself.

"My folks had a farm outside Leavenworth and there were eight of us. I was second to the oldest. Now you just keep in mind that Leavenworth was the first town in Kansas and that started the same year I was born. 1854 it was. Yes sir and the rest of Kansas was one open buffalo range. Well my Pa took sick and died and Ma had trouble feeding the herd of us. Was fourteen when I started ridin' the trails as a cow-hand. Figured it would be one less mouth for Ma to feed and I could save up my pay and send it back home to help.

"Used to steer the Texas Longhorn. Ahh, those were the good days. Nights out under the stars, cooking over a camp fire, and riding the open plain. I had a horse named 'Gypsy.' Good horse too.

"And then, one of the best parts of riding the trail was comin' to Dodge City. It was the heart of the wild frontier. Just about sprang up overnight. First store was built in '72.

"What do you need in a town? A few stores, a post office, a saloon, hotel, church, jail and school. Pick any three and ya got yourself a town. But no town ever grew faster and better than Dodge City.

"For those of us on the trail, we always looked forward to comin' in to town. You could get a hot meal of fancy fixins', a warm bath, a game of pool, stock up on cigars or any other necessities.

"Now, I know some folks think Dodge City was an evil, bad sort of place. That it weren't. Ladies and visitors were treated with great respect. Yes sir, chivalry was alive and well in good old Dodge City. Unless, of course, some one was looking for some kind of trouble, in which case he found it pretty darn quick.

"Gun fights, gambling, ladies of the evening – those were certainly part of this town. But there were some fine local folks who were real respectable-like. But we always warned the new cow-hands to stay south of the railroads if they had been drinking. Go north of Front Street and they'd slap you in jail real quick if you caused any disturbance that the genteel folk didn't like. But here on the south side, well that was another story.

"Those were the most glorious years," said the old timer wistfully, "for Dodge City and for me. But then in winter of '86 a huge blizzard came. Most of the cattle died. Men and horses died too. From there on out everything changed. Instead of cowboys herding the Texas Longhorns, ranchers built fences and kept their cattle on their own land. And Dodge City went from being the last town on the wild frontier to being a meat packing plant." His voice contorted as the last three words were forced from his mouth.

"What happened to you?" inquired Florence.

"Well, I was out of a job. So was every other cowboy I knew. Tried working in the meat packing plant."

Here the man spat on the ground. "Couldn't do it. Felt like I was a prisoner inside that plant."

"One day I says to myself, 'Jimmy, this ain't no life for a cowboy. I ain't never been a prisoner and I ain't gonna be one now.'

23

"So I hit the road. Instead of a cowboy, I became a hobo. Now I know some folks don't take too kindly to hobos. Think we're all lazy tramps. But truth be told, that was the only way I could find me some work. "

"Did seasonal work when I could find it. Always liked it best when I could work with horses and livestock, but I did just 'bout every kind of work a body could find. Wasn't quite the same as the days on the trail, but still it was a free life. Under the stars and not a care in the world. Unless the care was where you'd get yer next meal.

"Instead of a horse, I hopped the trains. Most hobos do, ya know. That's the only way one kin get from one place to the next. North to south. Town to country. I's seen it all.

"Two years ago as I was hopping off a train, my boot lace got stuck and I wasn't able to jump as far. Foot got run over by the train. My traveling days were over.

"There's a saying: 'Young hobos live by the trains but old hobos live in the camps.' When I recovered, I headed back to old Dodge City, the home of every real cowboy. And here I am."

Florence heard the baby start to whimper. She stood up. "Don't leave, I, I'll be right back."

Quickly she dashed into the shack to get the little one. "Hush, Martha. I'm here," she cooed to the baby. "We're going outside into the cool night air."

It had been so long since Florence had talked to anyone, she forgot how much she missed it. She carried the baby outside and settled back down on one of the crates.

Jimmy had lit a cigarette. The night was getting dark.

"So, Missy, tell me your story. How did you come to be in our hospitable camp here in Dodge?"

"I'm from Sherman, Kansas. My parents have a farm there."

"A farmer's daughter, huh?"

"Yes. Well," here she nodded to the baby in her arms. "When my parents found out, they kicked me out of the house."

"Well, now that happens too often. Oh no, don't have to get embarrassed with me. You're not the first or the last person that's happened to. 'Spect everyone here has known others in that predicament – and many of 'em has caused it. Don't pay no mind to what nobody else says."

"Always harder for women, says I," continued Jimmy. "Can't go hopping on and off trains with a baby in your arms. You got any plans?"

"I wrote a letter to my parents. I asked if I could go back home. I'm waiting to hear back," Florence confided.

"Yeah, I noticed yer hanging 'round the mess house when mail call comes. Don't give up hope now," Jimmy finished as he pushed himself up and reached for his crutches. "There's always a new day in Dodge City."

Florence watched as her new comrade limped away, the boot of his bad foot scraping the dirt path. He turned a corner at the end of a row of shanties.

From a distance, the voices of two or three men carried to her as Jimmy reached their hang out.

"Not been this hot since before the blizzard of '86," she heard him utter.

"What am I doing in a place like this?" Florence asked herself. "I don't want to be stuck here when I'm his age."

A rat was slinking across the path near her hut. Disgusted, she carried the baby inside, into the dark.

"We're gonna get out of here, Martha," she whispered to the baby. "One way or the other, we gotta get out."

***

25

Next morning, Florence woke as the sun was streaming through the cracks of her shanty. The baby was whimpering. Outside, sounds of camp life indicated others had already started their day.

She picked the baby up from the old wooden crate that was her crib. It was padded with a stack of newspapers Sarah had brought her for that purpose.

"Wonder if I can get some more newspapers. These are getting old." She made her meager plans for the coming day.

At noon, the young mother inconspicuously edged her way to the mess hall. Slowly she approached the man who seemed to be in charge. At various times, he brought items from Dodge City to the camp. As he caught her eye, he shook his head "no." Dejected, Florence left.

The next two days were the same. But the third day, she saw Jimmy limping toward her with an envelope in his hand.

"Good news, Missy," he called. "Letter came with your name on it. 'I'll take it to her,' says I. I know you've been awaiting for it."

Florence reached for the letter. Yes, those were her mother's distinct letters on the front. She tore the envelope open and held her breath, reading.

"Florence, We received your letter. As I clearly explained to you before, you cannot bring the baby to this house. You will need to make other arrangements."

Jimmy noted the expression on her face as she read.

"Well, now, I gather it ain't good news."

"No," Florence answered flatly, eyes shut.

A moment of silence hung in the hot, sulky air. The baby started to cry, sputtered, and spit up sour milk.

"That young 'un of yourn don't look too good," noted Jimmy. "I ain't no expert on babies now, but she seems kind of small and weak-like."

"I know."

"Best take her to Dr. Bronson."

"I don't have any money," Florence answered honestly.

"Don't matter," Jimmy responded. "He didn't charge you nuthin' when she was born, did he? He's stopped in to see me now and again and never charged a solitary dime. Some folks are like that, ya know. Lookin' to help others."

"Maybe," stated Florence absently, heading back to her shack.

Once inside, she closed the door, locking in the stale, hot air. Her shoulders shook as the sobs escaped.

Maybe she cried for ten minutes; maybe it was two hours. Back and forth she paced in the shack; now her prison cell. She only stopped as the baby coughed and spit up again.

She remembered what Jimmy said about the doctor. With a resigned sigh, she opened the door. There seemed nothing else to be done.

It was a short walk to the downtown area of the city. Her plan to ask for Dr. Bronson's house changed when she saw the sign on his door. Shoulders up, she climbed the stairs and knocked.

A middle age woman opened the door.

"Yes?"

"I'd like to see the doctor. My baby is sick."

"Come in, then," replied the woman, holding the door open further. "And you are?"

"My name is Florence. I'm from the camp by the river."

"I see, Florence. My name is Mrs. Bronson. My husband told me a baby was born there recently.

"May twelfth," Florence stated.

"Yes, then. That must have been you. Come in and have a seat. I'll let him know you are here."

After sitting, Florence watched the woman disappear through a door in the back. She ran her fingers over the fabric of the chair she sat on. Had she really lived in a house like this and sat in such a chair only a few months before?

Looking down, she noticed how tattered her dress was and her dusty shoes. A door opened. Footsteps approached. As the doctor drew near, she tried to hide her dirty fingernails.

"I understand the baby is not well," came the calm voice of the doctor.

"She's not eating. She kind of coughs; and throws up a lot."

The physician took the baby and unwrapped her.

"How old now?"

"Three weeks."

He listened with a stethoscope. His face looked serious as he looked into the mother's face.

"Young lady, what plans do you have?"

"I, I don't have any plans."

"Do you have family?"

"Yes." Briefly she told of the letter she received that day.

He was quiet for a few minutes. The grandfather clock ticked. The baby sputtered.

Finally he spoke. "Do you want your baby to live?"

"Of course," the mother stated.

"Well, then I need to be honest with you. She won't live. Not where you are currently staying."

"What am I to do?" Florence gasped.

"The only hope is to give her to someone who can feed her and take care of her properly."

"Do you know anyone who will take her?"

The doctor answered slowly. "I know everyone in Dodge City and most of the surrounding territory. Let me do some checking."

Florence stared at the floor through another long silence.

"I want my baby to live," she said finally.

"I'll be in touch," he answered.

***

A week later, Florence met Doctor Bronson at the courthouse. It was a large, intimidating building; a contrast from the quarters she had been staying in. On the door of the room they entered the judge's name was printed: "A.H. Preston, Probate Judge."

"Your name?" he asked.

"Florence Hefner."

"Age?"

"Sixteen"

"The child's name," he continued, as he filled out the legal document on his desk.

Florence's voice started to waiver. "Martha Hefner"

"Her age?"

"She was born May 12 of this year."

"And you are before me in the Court of Ford County, consenting to give custody of this child up for permanent adoption."

Florence nodded her head.

The judge peered at her above his glasses. "It is my understanding that you have found a family who wish to adopt this baby. Is that correct?"

Dr. Bronson spoke up. "Yes, there is a couple living just

outside of Dodge City, a Mr. and Mrs. Matthews. They will be here this afternoon to take the baby and fill out the papers for adoption."

"Very well, said the judge. He signed his name, dated it June 14, 1909, and stamped the document in front of them. He nodded his dismissal to Florence. She hadn't even signed the document.

Slowly, Florence handed the baby to the doctor, looking at her one last time. Then she turned to go.

"How will you get home to your folks?" the doctor asked.

"I don't know," she said as she reached the door. She walked down the courthouse steps and down the street.

No one ever saw her again.

Not This Baby

A tall man in dungarees stopped his mule at the end of the row he was plowing. He looked up at the blazing sun straight overhead as he brushed his bushy blonde hair back with one hand and mopped his forehead with the other.

"Lunchtime" he announced, as much to the mule as to himself.

Both headed toward the small white farmhouse a short distance away where water and refreshment awaited them. He quickly looped the mule's rope near the water trench in the yard then bounded up the creaking steps of the front porch. Before he opened the door of the house, he could hear a thin wail coming from upstairs.

"Effie," he called as he entered the kitchen, "why is that baby still crying?"

"I don't know!" came the exasperated reply of a young woman placing dishes on the table "That baby's cried all morning and there's nothing I could do to stop her."

"Well, didn't you try feeding her, or changing her, or somethin'?"

"Tried all of that," the woman responded. "Throwing up and crying is about all that baby is good for."

"Don't start that kind of talk again, Effie. We went through this last night."

"It's true, Edward," the woman said with a sigh as she sat

31

down. "I'd like to leave the house to go in the fields like you, just to get away from the noise."

"But you were the one that had your heart so set on us getting a baby," her husband reminded her.

"I know. But not this baby. It's been more than a week and I swear she's cried almost the entire week without stopping."

There was a moment of silence as ham and beans and biscuits were dished out.

"Edward," his wife quietly said, "don't you think we might have made a mistake?"

"No," came the sharp answer. "We waited and waited to have our own. Then when our baby died we waited longer. Then once you convinced me we should adopt a baby we waited even more. Don't understand how you can finally get a baby and want to get rid of her."

"It's 'cuz I can't do anything with her," Effie complained. "She cries during the day; she cries all night. Cries when I hold her and when I put her down. When I try to feed her she settles down for a minute then throws it all up. Then she starts crying all over again."

"Well, it seems to me that baby is in need of a mother who will take care of her and not just leave her upstairs to cry."The man retorted. "You wanted a baby, now you got yourself one and seems you ought to do more to take care of her."

"Well, then you try taking care of her," his wife shouted at him.

The man scraped his plate clean and swallowed the last bite in silence. Without a word he got up from the table, grabbed his hat hanging on the hook by the door, then let the screen door bang behind him as he crossed the front porch.

Alone in the kitchen, Effie buried her head in her hands.

She watched out the window as her husband untied the mule and headed back to the fields.

"We'll see. We'll just see," she muttered through clench teeth. She untied her apron and reached for her bonnet.

***

All the windows were open in the Dodge City court office. The sounds of carts and horses and an occasional car could be heard. The clerk swatted an annoying fly away. He looked up as the door opened.

A tall woman in a farm dress and bonnet entered carrying a baby.

"May I help you?" he asked as she approached.

"I have a child who is a ward of the state," the woman answered.

"A ward?" the clerk asked.

"Yes, she is illegitimate and has no one to take care of her."

"Oh, I remember you," the clerk said, his face lighting with recognition. "You and your husband were here a few weeks ago to adopt a baby."

"Ten days ago."

"Is this the baby, then?" asked the clerk.

"It is."

"Wait here. I'll see if we can talk to Judge Preston."

Half an hour later, Effie was sitting in the office of Judge Preston, the same one who had signed their adoption papers just ten days before. The judge looked at the papers in his hands, then glanced at her over his glasses.

"Mrs. Mathews, I understand there is a problem with the adoption."

"Yes, sir."

33

"It states on this form that you filled out that the child is in need of care. He adjusted his glasses, and read from the paper in front of him. "'Martha Hefner is a dependent and neglected child; Martha Hefner is abandoned by her parents, is destitute and homeless, dependent upon the public for support, has no proper parental care or guardianship.'" He looked at her over the paper he held. "These are your words about this infant?"

"That is correct."

"May I ask why you do not want to continue with this baby as your adopted child?"

Effie took a deep breath. "The child is inconsolable. She is sickly and does nothing but cry. We had waited to adopt a baby, but since she has come into our home my husband and I have been arguing and fighting. It just isn't working out."

"Hmmm, I see. You will be able to provide temporary shelter until we can make arrangements?"

"Yes, if necessary."

"Very well. This document states that this child is now a ward of the state of Kansas and as such is under state custody. Her name reverts back to the name at birth: Martha Hefner."

"I understand."

"Someone will be in contact in the next day or two to get the baby." With a wave of his hand he dismissed Effie.

Slowly Effie carried the sleeping baby out of the room, out of the foyer, and down the stairs. "Am I doing the right thing?" she wondered.

***

Back in the courthouse Judge Preston walked to the next office.

"Mrs. States, contact the Kansas Children's Home. Tell them we have an infant who is a ward of the state and in need of placement."

Violet States looked up at him. "Is it true this is the same child Dr. Bronson took last week?" she asked.

"It is true," the judge sighed. "Not sure," he added, "when this courthouse became a nursery."

A Wamego Farm

The quiet of the early evening was broken by a distinct chugging sound heard over the crickets and birds. A black car was making its way noisily up the dusty country road from the small village of Wamego in Waubansee County. Inside a nearby large Victorian farmhouse, the occupants heard the car coming.

"That must be Ernest Stewart's new Model T Ford," announced the gray haired gentleman to family members around him. Four teenage boys crowded around the window, eager to watch one of the only cars in the area.

"Now back away from the door," stated their prim looking mother who entered the living room. She was a middle aged woman with a high neckline and cameo brooch who dismissed the boys with a wave of her hand. As she opened the front door and stepped on to the porch to greet their visitor, he emerged from the automobile.

"Good evening, Dr. Stewart," the woman of the house called out. "I must say your Runabout has captured the attention of our sons."

The tall man with wire-rimmed spectacles in a dark vest gave the car a friendly pat as he walked past it. "Yes, it has attracted a bit of attention. These Model T's just came out last year but are already recognized everywhere. But I must say that it is mighty handy to have a car when I have to make house calls in the middle of the night."

"Of course, of course," the woman agreed with him as he joined them on the porch. "Would you like to come in? Or perhaps you would like to sit on the front porch and enjoy what little breeze we can get."

"Good to see you Mattie. You too Ed." The two men exchanged a firm handshake. "It would be great to sit out on your porch tonight."

As the three settled themselves on the comfortable furniture, a young woman who looked about twenty years of age came out in response to the woman's call.

"We will be visiting with Dr. Stewart on the front porch. Please bring three glasses of tea."

"Yes Ma'am," responded the departing figure.

"Heard there's been some mosquitoes bothering livestock west of here," remarked the visitor. "Have you had any problems with your farm, Ed?"

"No, can't say we have. Read about it in the paper though. Just the usual flies that comes with raising hogs," answered Ed, as he looked out towards his fields to the south of his house.

The three continued small talk about farming until their tea arrived. As the physician thoughtfully stirred his tea, he looked over at the husband.

"Ed and Mattie, the Kansas Children's Home asked me to visit you. I understand that the two of you signed papers requesting a child."

"Why, yes we did, Doctor," answered Mrs. Grimm.

"Several months ago," added her husband.

"That's right, it was April 22. You see we would like a little girl. As you know, we are not getting any younger."

Both gentlemen chuckled at this statement. "I mean, we

have five children," Mrs. Grimm continued. "Our nineteen year old daughter is the oldest of course, and the only girl. Then we had the four boys. So we thought we would like to have another daughter."

"I see," answered the doctor, "you do have a lovely family."

"We asked for a girl two to five years old," Mattie continued. Her face lit up. "Are you coming to see us about a little girl for us to adopt?"

"Not exactly," the doctor sighed. "The orphanage has your name because you requested a girl, but they have asked me to see you about a slightly different matter."

Two sets of eyes waited expectantly for him to continue.

"You see," Dr. Stewart continued, "there are no children that meet your description at this time. However, there is a two month old who is need of a home."

"Two months!" responded Mrs. Grimm. "That's really an infant. We were planning on a child a little older than that."

"I understand," replied the doctor.

"But tell us more about this baby, if you will," added the quiet voice of Mr. Grimm.

"Well, here's the story Ed. I got a telegram today all the way from Dodge City. There is a two month old who is a ward of the state of Kansas. Seems they are having trouble finding anyone to keep her. They would put her in the orphanage except it is full and they don't have enough workers to take care of another baby."

"That's very troubling," remarked the woman.

"Indeed it is Plus I need to let you know that this baby is not in good health. Not at all. They are looking for a family who can take care of her for the immediate time being. Since you had applied for a child, I was asked to see if you would be willing to take this infant in, even though she is not the age you requested."

"Why, of course we would consider it our duty to offer this child shelter," replied the woman without consulting her husband. One look at the kindly eyes of the quiet farmer by her side assured the physician that he agreed with his wife.

"I'm very glad you are willing to take the child in," stated Dr. Stewart. "I will send a telegram to Dodge City tonight. I anticipate they will be sending the infant by train in a few days. It is probably an eight hour trip by train to bring her here."

"We would be able to meet the train as soon as we hear that she has arrived," stated the gentleman.

"This is a big relief," replied the doctor as he stood to go. "I want to get back to town and get that telegram sent right away. As I said, they are having a hard time finding shelter for this little one."

Ed and Mattie walked the physician to his car.

"By the way," asked Mattie as he was getting in his car, "do you have any idea how long we will be keeping this child before more permanent arrangements can be made for her."

"I don't think it will be terribly long." The doctor answered from the rolled down window of his Runabout. "From what I understand, the child is not expected to live."

The Eskridge Reunion

1928

Hazel finished putting on her eye-liner and looked closely at her reflection in the mirror. She was a beautiful brunette of about 19 years with short bobbed, naturally curly hair. Her hazel colored eyes indicated where she got her name. She turned side-ways to look at her figure in her flapper dress.

Her reflection smiled back at her, satisfied with the picture she made. Her dress was the latest style: broad shoulders, straight cut, shimmering red fabric, and calf-length hem. Below the hem shiny rayon stockings and high-heeled shoes were seen. The matching bandeau around her head perfected her outfit.

"Not bad," Hazel stated to her reflection. "Not bad at all. And since tonight may be my one and only chance, this isn't such a bad start."

She compared the outfit in the mirror to the dress which adorned her older sister in a black and white portrait on her bureau. "The 1920's sure have made a big change in fashion," she thought to herself. Until recently it was the wealthy women who had dictated what was stylish. But that had changed. The flappers of the 1920's were middle class women with their own bold statements to make causing a permanent change in fashion. No longer would the wealthy decide what constituted style.

This was a good thing for Hazel. She had been raised in

comfort. While her family was not exactly wealthy, their prosperous farm had easily met all their needs and contributed handsomely to obtaining most of their wants when she was a girl. Though recent hard times had ruined the family's income, it hadn't changed her beauty. Or her style.

She picked up her handbag, gave a last approving nod at the mirror, and headed to the hall way. Down the stairs, she overheard her mother and older sister discussing their garden vegetables. "How mundane," she thought to herself as she slipped out the door.

Nathan was waiting in the driveway. Saturday nights Nathan or one of her other brothers would drop her off in town. Most of the farming community came to town Saturday night. There they would sell their eggs and cream and pick up supplies they wanted at the farm. It gave everyone in the community a chance to socialize.

The older brother eyed Hazel when she slipped into the car next to him. "Pretty fancy looking dress to go into town to sell eggs, Little Sister."

"Oh, you mean this dress?" Hazel responded. "It's the high school reunion tonight. I thought I would head over there, instead. "

"Umm huh," he muttered as the car headed down the road. After a few moments he spoke up again. "Seems to me just about this time last year you were more than pleased to be done with school and you all were anxious to go your separate ways."

"Of course," Hazel answered nonchalantly. "Everyone wants to graduate and get out of school." Hazel tried to keep her explanations neutral. The last thing she wanted was for Nathan to suspect her real goal in attending her reunion tonight. "But it doesn't mean I don't want to ever see them again."

Nathan slowed his car as they approached the high school.

"Thanks," Hazel called as she opened the door. "And you don't need to pick me up. I can catch a ride with someone else." The car pulled away, and Hazel turned to face her old high school.

Last year they had graduated: the Eskridge High School class of 1927. Tonight the eighteen former classmates would be back together again, to laugh and dance and celebrate their first year of official adulthood "Almost everyone will be here," she thought to herself. "Particularly Carlton."

Opening the door of the high school brought back memories of the four years Hazel spent studying and socializing. She started toward the gymnasium and could hear the music even before she got half way down the hall.

Four others from her class were already there. She heard her name called and quickly joined them near the gramophone. It seemed like only a few minutes and most of the others were there.

Hazel mingled easily with her old classmates but her eyes often returned to Carlton, standing in the corner. He looked tall and regal in his pin striped suit. Her ears frequently picked out his low laugh. As inconspicuously as possible, Hazel made her way toward a cluster of three people which included Carlton.

"Good evening, Ann. Hi Carlton. Saw you in your new car, Howard," Hazel greeted the others.

"Hey there, Hazel," Carlton responded. Ann turned and eyed Hazel's outfit. But it was the man she called Howard who had the most to say.

"Well, now Hazel, that outfit sure is more stunning than what you used to wear to class," remarked the easy going Howard.

Hazel joined the laughter with the others.

42

"So tell me, Hazel," began Ann, "how do you like living closer to Eskridge? Do you prefer living in town or would you rather still be way out in the country?"

A tense moment followed while the two men waited to see how Hazel would handle the bait. Everyone in the class was aware that her family's hogs had died from a sudden, contagious illness, forcing her family to move to a smaller farm just two miles from the town of Eskridge.

"I want to be where ever the party is," Hazel brushed aside the jibe. "Hey, that's Duke Ellington's latest song they are playing on the gramophone." She looked over at Carlton. "Do you know the Sugar Step dance, Carlton?"

"Well, I've tried it a few times, but I'm no expert", he began tentatively.

"Oh I know it, Carlton." Ann chimed in quickly. "I know it real well. Come on, I'll show you." Ann took Carlton by the arm and together they started toward the dance floor. Hazel noticed the triumphant look that Ann flashed her over her shoulder.

"Looks like you'll have to dance the Sugar Step with me," Howard said when the two had walked away.

"Okay, Howard," Hazel replied. "Let's see how well you can do the Sugar Step."

The dance lasted a few minutes and Howard kept perfect timing. After it was done, Hazel stated breathlessly, "I have to say I'm surprised, Howard. I didn't know you could dance so well."

"Shhh," Howard chuckled. "Don't say it so loud my dear mother hears you. She never approved of dancing."

Hazel chuckled with him. Everyone in the class knew that Howard's mother was a kind, gentle woman who adhered strictly to a faith her brash, impetuous son did not share.

43

They made their way to the punch bowl where a larger group had gathered. Hazel flashed a vibrant smile to the quiet Delbert who was serving his former classmates a pink-colored beverage. She began a conversation with Tommy Burton about his new car. She pretended to be interested, but kept her eye on Carlton. He and Ann were walking together toward the table of refreshments.

Hazel laughed gleefully about Tommy's story.

"Hey guys," she called to the group at the table, "you should hear how Tommy ran out of gas in a thunderstorm. "

As the night went on, Hazel chatted with everyone in the class. She danced with four or five different guys, but not Carlton. He was friendly when she spoke to him, but no more.

Tommy was by the gramophone changing records when someone called out, "Put the Charleston on Tommy!"

"Sure," he responded with a grin. From the machine came the fast jazz sounds of the famous song from Charleston which had blazed across the country. Tommy winked at Hazel and crossed over to her. Together they started the upbeat bouncing steps as other dancers joined them on the floor.

Forward, backward, cross in front. Hazel knew the popular dance well and even in her heels could stay on the balls of her feet. Her arms flailed to the front and side in perfect time with the one-and-two, three-and-four rhythm of her feet. It was that distinct arm motion of her and her friends in the room that caused the dancers of the roaring twenties to be called flappers.

After several moments, Tommy started to laugh. "Sorry, Hazel, that's all I know."

"I can finish," came a voice near-by. To her left, Howard stepped to her side, and without missing a beat the dance continued.

44

Moment by moment other dancers dropped out until the only two couples still on the floor were Hazel with Howard and Carlton with Ann. The others crowded around, cheering and cat-calling as the more complicated steps were done by the confident dancers.

As the dancers crisscrossed back and forth, Carlton passed Hazel and panted, "I'm glad Cecil Johnson's song only lasts four minutes."

"Oh, I could do this all night," she called back.

Now came the trickiest part of the dance. Around the World was a kick to the front and side followed by a 180 degree turn that had to be done without losing time to the quick beat.

Hazel heard Ann groan and the crowd laugh half-way through the turn. She didn't dare look for fear of missing a beat herself, but Hazel rightly guessed that Ann had not been able to execute the demanding turn.

"Go for it, Howard," Carlton called, "looks like we're out."

Hazel was breathless but happy. Encouraged by the clapping and cheers, their steps became more energetic as they danced side by side. Kick to the side, two steps up – one step back, the moves continued.

"Gotta get this one right" Hazel thought as the final high circular kick came. More cheers. As the song ended, laughter and applause surrounded them.

Tommy slapped both Hazel and Howard on the back. "Now that's what I call dancing," he said.

"Thanks," Hazel laughed, "but I think you're the one that started it."

Carlton marched over to join them. "Good job. You two ought to form a dance team. What do you think everybody," he called in a louder voice to the group, "The Eskridge High Dancing Duo."

"Well," said Hazel glancing at her watch, "this part of the duo better get herself home before it gets any later."

She noticed a few others had started to grab their things. Carlton helped Ann put on her shawl. Hazel groaned inside.

"Hazel, do you have a ride?" asked Howard.

"Was hoping to catch one," she answered.

"I'll take you home."

"That would be swell," Hazel responded, noticing from the corner of her eye that Carlton and Ann were leaving together.

She called her good-byes to a few other friends and headed to his car. He held the front passenger door open for her, then got in on the driver's side.

"Didn't know you could dance so well," she told him again.

"Actually," Howard stated, "I have to admit I prefer old fashioned square dancing to jazz and the Charleston."

"Really?"

"Sure do. With square dancing everyone can join in, everyone can learn the calls, and everyone is doing the same thing. Wouldn't mind being a square dance caller myself."

"You would rather do the calling than the dancing?" she asked him.

"Like to do both. So, what kind of music and dancing do you like best," he inquired.

"I like them all," she stated honestly. "I've been playing the piano ever since I can remember. I like all kinds of music."

"Would you rather play or dance?" he asked.

"Probably dance. But don't tell my mother."

"We both seem to have that in common," Howard laughed. "We have to sneak out of the house to dance."

"But my mother encourages piano playing," she explained. "And I really do like playing when I am at home alone.

46

My father talked about buying me a grand piano. But then our hogs caught disease and of course we lost the farm and there went the plans for a grand piano. But my sister's upright is high quality. It's good enough. I mean it has to be now."

"Bet it sounds good when you play it."

"I like to think it does," she answered. "I don't plan on becoming a musician or anything. I just like to play sometimes."

They had reached her house.

"Well then," Howard said pulling his car into her driveway, "I'd like to hear you play sometime. Thanks for dancing tonight."

"It was fun," Hazel called to him before closing the door. She watched him back his car up and drive away.

"It really was fun," she thought to herself as she opened the door of her house. "But I wonder if Carlton cares as much for Ann as she obviously does for him." She closed the door behind her with a firm click.

"Hazel Marie Grimm" came a sharp voice. Her mother stood back behind the window, a corner of the curtain in her hand. "What do you mean coming home this time of night? And with a boy no less!"

"Why, I've been to my class reunion at the high school," the daughter replied.

"At this hour?" demanded her mother, arms folded across her chest.

"It's only ten o'clock," Hazel replied defensively. "I didn't leave any later than anyone else."

"Do not talk back to me. I cannot believe you would disgrace our family by being out late at night like this. Do you even think of our family's reputation?"

Hazel stared at her mother.

"Do you know what your sister has gone through because

47

of you?"

"Wh- what?"Hazel asked, confusion showing in her face.

"I guess it is high time you find out." Her mother's high pitched voice was strained with tension. "Your father and I are not your parents!"

"What?" Hazel asked again, looking straight into the angry eyes of the gray-haired woman standing before her.

"We took you in when you were a baby," continued the woman. "You had no family. You had nothing. You weren't even expected to live. But we took you in and gave you a chance in life. And this is how you repay us?"

Slowly Hazel lowered herself onto the sofa.

"Think about what this has done to Cora's reputation. She was nineteen years old and all of a sudden we have a baby in the house. For years others have whispered behind your sister's back that she is your mother. But you had no mother."

Hazel stared at the floor. "I wondered what they meant," she whispered.

"Who?" her mother asked. "What do you mean?"

"My classmates. We were children."

Hazel closed her eyes as a memory of children playing in the school yard returned. The very same classmates she had just danced and partied with half an hour before. But it happened ten years ago. Wasn't it Little Tommy Burton who had said those words that had frequently haunted her?

"Don't pay her no mind," he had said to the rest of the kids."She's adopted. She ain't got no real folks."

It had surprised Hazel when she heard it, but none of the other children had listened to Tommy. His words evaporated in thin air as the young scholars had chased around the one-room school yard, unaffected by what he said. But Hazel had heard. And wondered.

"That's what the kids meant when they said I didn't have any real folks?" Hazel said, eyes still fixed on the floor.

"What kids? What did you hear?" her mother pried.

Hazel recounted the incident on the playground years before.

"I wondered why he said that. And I wondered why my parents were older than everyone else's parents."

"Well, so did a lot of other people," replied Mrs. Grimm, a little calmer than before. "Perhaps I should have told you before now. But all these years Cora's reputation has been tarnished because we adopted you. And the very least you could do is think of the family name when you decide to stay out partying all night long."

Slowly Hazel stood to her feet. Numbly she climbed the stairs and passed Cora in the hallway. Cora looked at her sadly and reached out to her. But Hazel walked past.

Cora: the older sister who had really been the one who raised her. It had always been Cora who dressed her, and read to her, and came when she called. "Is it true her reputation was ruined because I exist?" thought Hazel.

She entered her room, closed the door, and leaned against it. "Why didn't they tell me sooner," she asked silently.

But she knew why. Adopted children were considered inferior by some people and parents often sought to hide the status of their adopted children, even from the child. She had heard stories of adults discovering their adoption when going through the papers of their deceased parents. The fear of learning one was adopted was a ghost that haunted many, whether real or not. Well the ghost was out.

She looked around the bedroom. There in the mirror was her reflection. The outfit was the same as the one in the looking glass several hours ago; but the face had changed. Then the eyes were filled with expectation and hope. Now they simmered with anger.

"Well, if that's what they think of me, I don't have to stay in this family any longer."

She looked over at the wall and the photo of her high school class hanging there. As always, her eyes went to the picture of Carlton.

"There doesn't seem to be much hope there," she thought as her mind replayed the events of the night. Then her eyes moved over a few inches.

"Howard?" She thought for a moment. "Yes, Howard. He will be my ticket out of here."

Tornado!

1941

A light breeze stirred the sheets hanging on the line. Hazel added another shirt and took a step to the next section of the clothes line. Between the diapers and blue jeans and towels, the light of the midday sun made an odd arrangement of shadows on the ground.

She sighed as she thought of her high school reunion coming in only a few days. Fourteen years ago, she thought. And for the last eleven she had been married to Howard.

Howard. She bit her lip as she thought of him. No, it wasn't like their marriage had been a perfect one. But she never expected he would do this. She thought back to their relatively brief courtship. But before they got married the whole world had changed. The stock market crash of 1929 had sent the world into an economic depression.

They got married anyway. It didn't seem at the time that a few local banks failing should prevent their wedding plans. How little did either of them know how hard it would be to raise a family when work and food were scarce. And then there were the kids. One by one the children came: first Bill, her oldest child. Then they had a little girl. She glanced over at her daughter playing with her doll under the tree. And now the baby, Dick, sleeping nearby in his cradle. Hazel's dreams had been smothered beneath dishes and laundry. But even those were better than what she faced now.

"It hasn't all been bad," thought Hazel, adding a pillow case to the line. They both had family in Eskridge and visited often. Life here in Topeka had its advantages. She and Howard still enjoyed music and dancing and there was plenty of opportunity in the city. In exchange for some light carpentry work that Howard did, they were able to go ball room dancing every week. But that's when they met Lenora. Hazel gritted her teeth as she remembered.

Half the clothes in her basket were hung when a brisk wind came up, flapping the clothes line that had been still minutes before. "Where did that come from?" Hazel wondered. Before she got to the end of the line she noticed a darkening sky. The wind increased in strength.

"On no," she groaned. "All this work and now the laundry is going to get rained on." Another look at the sky and her concern for the clothes vanished. Gray clouds were moving quickly to cover the sky that was sun-filled only minutes before. The lashing wind blew the trash can over and it rolled toward her as the sounds of the coming storm grew.

"Get to the cellar," she yelled to her seven year old daughter playing with her doll nearby. She ran to the cradle to pick up the baby.

"Bill," yelled the mother. "Bill, where are you?"

No answer was heard.

"Bill!" she yelled again. "Where is he?" she asked her daughter, "Where did your brother go?"

The little girl looked up at her with frightened eyes. She pointed to the end of the house. "He went that way," she stated.

The mother grabbed her ten month old, now awake and crying. "Come on, we have to get the two of you to the cellar."

Bent double against the wind, the baby in one arm and dragging the frightened child with the other hand, she edged

52

toward the house. The wind whipped the clothes line from the pole. Tangled in a nest of clothes, Hazel tripped. She barely managed to stay on her feet, but found her daughter sprawled on the ground in front of her.

"My doll," the little girl started to cry as the wind snatched it from her.

"Never mind the doll. Get up quick!"

The line was untangled and once more she pulled her children toward the cellar of the house as a torrential rain dumped water from the sky.

"Bill," Hazel yelled even louder. She could barely hear herself yelling over the sound of the storm's fury.

"My doll," the little girl wailed again. Clothes, pots, toys were blown across the yard and their neighbors belongings were wildly rolling through theirs.

Right then she saw her oldest son coming around the corner, pushed by the wind. He bent over for just a second, picked up his sister's doll and sprinted toward his mother.

She struggled with the latch on the cellar. As she pulled the wooden door open, the musty odor from inside met her. "Into the cellar! Now!" their mother yelled.

In two leaps the boy was down the stairs, pulling his sister with him. Hazel followed with the baby and drew the cellar door shut. Trembling, she made her way down the stairs to her children and slumped on the bottom step. Donna reached for the wet doll her brother had let fall to the floor.

"Wow, that sure came up fast," the older brother exclaimed.

"Where had you been? I was calling for you and didn't see you?"

"Me and the guys went to the corner lot to play marbles," he answered. "It was all hot and sunny, and then all of the sudden the sky got dark and wind was blowing everything around.

So I ran home. I wonder if the other guys made it home."

"I sure hope so."

Outside the storm was gathering strength. A loud crash was heard.

"What was that?" the little girl asked, eyes wide.

"I think a tree might have fallen," the mother responded, trying to keep her voice calm. "Don't know if it was just a large branch or the whole tree."

"Must be a big tornado," Bill guessed.

"Yes, I think it is," his mother agreed. Hazel thought back to the many tornadoes she had lived through. She recalled her mother calmly standing in their front yard pointing to twisters across the field. "But I sure don't remember any coming up this fast."

"Where's Daddy?" the daughter asked.

"He's not here," her mother answered.

A crash of thunder and bolt of lightning jolted all of them. The baby buried his head on his mother's chest as his sister grabbed hold of her arm. Even the older brother jumped closer to her; then backed off.

"I can tell Dad is not here," the boy returned. "But where is he now?"

"He's in Kansas City right now."

"When is he coming back?"

Hazel buried her face in the baby's neck. How was she going to tell them?

"I said 'When is he coming back?' " Bill asked again.

In the silence of the cellar, the three could hear the wind outside. Hazel heard the baby breathing as she tried to think of what to say.

Did she have to tell them? Until now, no one suspected

anything. It was normal for Howard to be away working. He had delivered milk for Kroeger Dairy Farm for a while. It didn't pay him money but it did provide them with all the milk and dairy products they needed. He worked in construction, moving from Topeka to Wichita, anywhere he could get work. He had been a hard worker, she would grant him that.

Over the years of the Depression he worked many odd jobs. Relatives on the farms provided food and he had helped there when help was needed. Bit by bit, they struggled through those lean years finding a little money here, a little food or housing there. He had provided for them then. But that was then. That was before he met Lenora.

Hazel kept her face buried in the baby's neck. "I'm not going to tell them," she said to herself. "I'm not going to be the one that tells them their father is never coming home again."

Part 2

The Deer & The Antelope

Hello, Kansas

1948

"Look! Look at him go!"

Excited voices around Donna aroused her from her sleep. The jostling and chugging of the train continued, but she gradually became aware the other passengers were watching something outside. She slowly raised her head to look out the window.

She saw an open field in the bright rays of the midday sun. Sprinting across the field was a sand-colored antelope. With his antlers held high, he galloped across the plain, parallel to the railroad tracks.

Donna smiled at the animal. She glanced to see if there were other members of a herd nearby. She saw none. Her eyes returned to the solitary male racing a modern train charging across his territory.

Showing off his speed and agility, the antelope pulled ahead of the train. The passengers laughed and applauded. Donna found she was clapping too.

"It's a pronghorn antelope," stated a gruff, male voice behind her. "Fastest animal in America, he is. Lots of 'em in Western Kansas, but don't see that many this far to the east of the state."

"So we are in Kansas now," Donna reflected as the antelope raced out of sight of her window. She glanced at her watch.

More than thirty-one hours had passed since her father and step-mother had watched her board the train in Boston. "Only forty five more minutes to go. Wonder who will be there to meet me."

Donna's knees jiggled impatiently this last part of the journey. She glanced down at her purse carrying the pictures of those she loved, then closed her eyes as she unconsciously twirled her hair around her finger and recounted again to herself what she hoped to gain in the next few weeks. See all her relatives, yes. Discover what happened to pull her parents apart and her half a continent away from her brothers. And find a way she might be reunited with her mother. That last one, she knew, would be the hardest.

The slowing of the train indicated they were approaching the station. Donna scanned the crowd. There. She spotted Aunt Cora in an old-fashion blue dress, her long hair pulled into a tight bun.

She alighted from the train, holding back the urge to push through the slower moving passengers in front of her. She made her way across the platform and flung herself into Aunt Cora's arms. But it wasn't Cora's voice she heard first.

"There you are, Donna. My haven't you grown."

Above all the noises on the platform, Donna heard her mother's voice. She let go of Cora and turned around. Her eyes opened wide at the site of her mother.

"She's even prettier than I remember," Donna thought. She looked at her mother's large eyes, stylish hair, and pink dress.

"Hi, Mother," Donna stated simply, silently wondering how someone who looked so friendly had stirred up such hatred in others.

Her mother kissed her cheek. "Bet you are tired from your long journey."

Uncle Nathan jingled his keys as Donna turned to greet him. "Let's find your luggage and get on home," he said. "Cora's been cooking all day, waiting for you to get here."

The party of four made their way to Nathan's car. Donna sat in the back with her mother, answering questions and pointing out familiar sites as the car passed. Nathan slowed the car down as they entered the city limits of Eskridge, easily marked by the concrete road going through Main Street. The town was only a couple of blocks long, a bank on each end of the street and a row of plain looking stores and buildings in between.

"Reminds me of a scene from the Wild West," she remarked out loud.

"This was the Wild West, at least at one time," her uncle remarked. "But it's pretty tame now," he added. Leaving the town, he turned onto a country lane with an oil and gravel road. It was a short ride to Nathan and Cora's home. As the car drew up, she jumped out. Nathan headed toward the house with her suitcase, but Donna lingered a moment to stare at the Victorian farmhouse and old barn and out buildings.

"Can I go see Tony right now?" she asked eagerly.

"In your dress and heels?" her mother asked.

"Better get changed first," Aunt Cora answered. "I thought you would be rearing to see him."

Donna bolted toward the house, eager to put on pants and head toward the barn. But once in the house she skidded to a stop.

Closing her eyes she inhaled deeply, savoring the almost-forgotten aromas of Aunt Cora's home, feeling like she had stepped across a threshold to another time. The world had moved forward, but here on the farm it had stood still.

"No electricity," she remembered, silently eyeing the kerosene lamp on the old-fashioned table. The wooden furniture was simple. The linoleum was a severe contrast to Kithy and Marion's carpets but far more efficient in fighting the scads of Kansas soil that inevitably found its way from the farmyard to the farmhouse floor.

At a slower pace she headed toward her room, touching the faded wall paper, noting the old black pot belly stove in the corner, out of the way and unneeded in July, but ready for the cold winters that unalterably followed the summer months.

She entered her old bedroom and shut the door. Uncle Nathan already had her luggage on the floor. But she didn't reach for it. Not yet. She looked lovingly around the room. The bedspread was done neatly, the organdy curtains were flapping in the slight breeze. Yes, Cora would have remembered to open the curtains and air out the room for her.

There on the wicker chair was her doll, Betsy. She crossed the room and picked her up. Had Aunt Cora sat the doll in the chair thinking Donna would still play with her? No, Cora would know she didn't play dolls anymore. Donna stroked the well-worn dress and smiled as she realized this was simply where Cora thought Betsy belonged: sitting in Donna's old room waiting where she had been left.

Donna tossed her travel clothes on the bed as she donned her pants and shirt. She raced out of her room, down the hall, and across the yard slamming the door. This reminded her of another difference from her New England home where no one would think of running in the house or slamming doors. But she had no worry of being scolded by Aunt Cora.

Crossing into the darkness of the barn Donna called, "Tony." She heard his answering neigh before she could see the bay pony in the corner. She approached his stall. "Hey, Tony, I'm here. I couldn't wait to see you."

She threw her arms around his neck, wishing she hadn't

run out of the house before getting him a carrot or apple from the kitchen. Her fingers stroked his mane. "You do remember me, don't you?" she repeated, certain her horse wouldn't forget her any more than she would forget him. She called a friendly greeting to Old Blue, Aunt Cora's mottled gray farm horse who stuck her head across the gate toward Donna. But she didn't leave Tony's side.

"Not as young as he used to be."

She hadn't realized Uncle Nathan was in the stable.

"Can I ride him now?"

"Well, don't see why not," he answered slowly. "But you need to be careful with him in this heat. He's not been feeling well lately."

"Is something wrong?"

"Well, can't say if he's sick or just getting old," her uncle answered. "Maybe he just doesn't like this heat any more than the rest of us."

"But is he ok?"

"Time'll tell," answered Uncle Nathan as he carried the smaller saddle to Tony's stall. "But as long as you ride him gently and not too long in the hot sun, I think he'll be all right."

Donna contemplated his words as the two got the pony saddled. She didn't remember ever being cautioned to ride gently or not too long. As she climbed into the saddle she looked again at Nathan.

"Uncle, are you sure he's going to be okay?"

"Nope I can't be sure." In response to her worried look he added, "None of us is getting any younger; him, you or me." He lightly swatted Tony's rump to get him headed out outside.

As the pony began their trip, Donna recognized a change. Tony moved slower and with less energy. Could he be getting sick? Or simply old?

Across the field, Tony walked. Donna held back the urge to nudge him into a canter. In one of her last letters Cora had mentioned Tony wasn't eating as much. But if he was sick, why didn't they tell her?

"It's not fair." Unbidden the words came to her mind.

Like the doll Betsy, Tony was supposed to always be there waiting for her to ride. The farm house, Cora, even the old kerosene heater: they belonged to her and should remain, a changeless island in a world of constant changes.

"None of us is getting any younger," she remembered her uncle's voice. For a brief instant a thought flickered through her mind. Her horse and her family were not like her doll, sitting unchanged with a perpetual smile on her face. While Donna was on the other side of the country, getting older, learning new things, was it possible that those she left behind in Kansas were also changing?

"Maybe Tony's just sick and will get better," she consoled herself. But thinking he might be sick didn't relieve her anxiety. How could she make sure he got better?

Someone ought to know - like a horse veterinarian. There was one in Eskridge, she knew. But, of course, vets cost money and Aunt Cora and Uncle Nathan did not have much money. She couldn't ask them to get a vet to come see Tony.

As the old gong rang, Donna turned Tony back toward the stable. Cora looked on knowingly as a more subdued Donna joined her in the farmhouse kitchen. As she washed her hands at the sink, her aunt handed her a dish towel to dry her hands. Donna recognized the old frayed towel she had dried many a dish with in her younger years. She looked around. The spoon holder hanging on the wall, the oil cloth on the table, even the old salt and pepper shakers seemed like priceless treasures from her store of childhood memories. Simultaneously she noted they were old and worn.

So different from Kithy and Marion's kitchen, Donna noted. She wasn't trying to make comparisons between her aunt's kitchen and step-mother's, but it was impossible not to. The plain and mismatched dishes were the opposite of Marion and Kithy's New England china. But here in Cora's kitchen things were plain and simple.

As dishes were passed, Donna described the antelope seen from the train. Uncle Nathan was quite interested.

"Must have been a young stag," he declared. "They can be a bit competitive when a car or horse is in their territory. Apparently trains too. They like to think they're the boss so they show off how fast they can run."

"How come?"

"Because they can," he answered.

That reminded her of Tony.

"Is Tony sick?" she asked. "I mean, he walks much slower than before."

The table was silent for a moment. It was Cora who spoke first.

"We have noticed he's not doing well, not eating with a healthy appetite. Ponies are like all other living things, sometimes they get sick. And then sometimes they get old."

"Is he sick or old?"

"We are not sure, Honey. Maybe a little of both. We'll just keep feeding him well and see if a good diet and fresh sunshine won't make him better, hmm? "

Donna bit her tongue to hold back from asking about getting a vet. But she saw Cora's eyes and knew Cora knew what she was thinking.

"Oh, I'm sure he'll be all right," her mother said. Donna glanced at her mother without feeling reassured. It really wouldn't be like her to worry about a horse too much one way or the other, Donna thought.

"Maybe you can ask your Grandpa Hogue tonight," her mother continued. "He's raised and cared for many farm animals in his time."

Donna looked over at her mother. "Grandma and Grandpa Hogue! Tonight?"

Cora smiled at Donna's enthusiasm at the news. "As much as we would love to have you all to ourselves, your father's parents want to see you too. They asked if you could come over to their farm for dinner tonight."

It was just like her aunt; always ready to share everything she had. Even Donna.

Uncle Nathan headed back to the barn, while Donna lingered a little longer at the table with Mother and Aunt Cora.

"I'll be heading back to my apartment in Topeka here soon," Mother was saying. "But I wanted to make sure I was here to greet you when your train arrived."

"You aren't staying, Mother?"

Cora chuckled. "It's no secret your mother prefers Topeka to the farm."

"I can't deny it," her mother laughed. "I must admit I'm a bit partial to running water, flushing toilets, and my electric fan on these hot July days. But you and Bill have always taken a liking to farm life."

"And Aunt Cora," her daughter added She and her aunt exchanged smiles.

"Yes, indeed, and Aunt Cora. And Uncle Nathan, and your pony. Not to mention your other grandparents. No, I don't blame you for wanting to stay out here with Cora on the farm. That's why we've arranged for you to spend a few weeks here. But," her mother added, "I've taken time off of work so when you do come out to Topeka we can spend some time together."

"Great," her daughter answered cheerfully. She nodded, inwardly relieved that her visit would include time for her and her mother to be alone together.

"But you know," her mother continued, "I really wish you and your brother Bill could have visited together. It was your father who planned that you should come to Kansas for a visit while Bill went to Massachusetts. Seemed to me that the two of you would want some time together."

Donna saw Aunt Cora nod her head and she silently agreed with them. Bill had arrived in Massachusetts only a short time before she had left for Kansas.

She saw her mother reach for her purse.

"Are you leaving already?" she asked in surprise.

Mother pulled out her mirror and lipstick which she applied while answering. "I need to get back on the road. I'm going to dinner and a movie with Louis tonight, and I don't want to be late."

"Louis?"

"Oh, he's a gentleman I met. He wants to meet you when you come to stay with me in Topeka."

Donna didn't know what to say. She glanced at Cora whose kind face was expressionless.

"I guess that's why she doesn't care I'm spending tonight with Dad's parents," Donna speculated silently. "Seems she's got plans of her own." But she also noted her mother said "when you come to stay with me in Topeka."

It made her feel hopeful.

***

After Mother's departure, Donna spent the afternoon

talking with Cora in the house, following Uncle Nathan around the farm, and riding Tony. It seemed a short time before Nathan announced that it was time to head to the Hogue farm for dinner. She hugged Aunt Cora good-bye and cheerfully climbed into the car next to her uncle. In spite of her anticipation of seeing her grandparents, Donna reminded herself that she wanted this to me more than a vacation.

"Thanks for driving me over, Uncle Nathan," she said when they were alone in his pick-up truck.

"Not a problem."

"You know," she added as the truck headed down the gravel road, "you must have driven Bill and me back and forth between your farm and Grandma and Grandpa Hogue's farm hundreds of times."

"Probably."

"Bill sure loves the farm you know."

She saw her uncle smile and nod. "You know what Bill said when my Dad called and asked him to come out to Massachusetts for the summer?"

"What?" Nathan responded.

"Bill said 'no.' He told my father he wouldn't leave Kansas unless my Dad promised him he would be coming back to live with Grandma and Grandpa and could continue going to school here in Eskridge. Can you believe he said that?"

"Uh huh," her uncle answered. "I'm not at all surprised your brother insisted on staying in Kansas."

Donna chortled. "I don't hear too many people saying 'No' to Dad. I'd never get away with it." The two were silent a moment. "But you know what Bill told me when he got to Massachusetts last month?"

"What?"

"He told me he didn't like how Dad had decided I was

68

going to live in Massachusetts and took me away from here. I didn't mind, at least not at the time. But Bill minded it. That's why he didn't want to go back to see Dad at first. But I was sure glad he agreed to come out for a summer visit."

"I imagine you were happy to see him."

"Oh I was, Uncle Nathan, I really was. In fact…"

"In fact what?" her uncle queried?

"I cried," Donna answered sheepishly. She saw her uncle glance at her from the corner of her eye. "I know it sounds stupid," she continued, "but I cried because I was so happy, just like I did when Dad came back from the war. I mean, it's not like my brother was in a war or anything. But when he got off the plane I ran up to him and started crying."

"That's because you've missed him."

"Yes, I've missed him. I've missed all of you the last two years. But you know what's funny?"

"What?" her uncle patiently asked.

I'm here at Bill's home in Eskridge and now he's back at my home in Massachusetts. Isn't that strange?"

"It's called summer vacation. That's when kids go visiting."

"I guess," Donna answered. She looked at her uncle more closely, wondering if he might help persuade her father to let her stay in Kansas. Uncle Nathan was a man of few words, strict but not unkind. Studious and well educated, he preferred books to conversation.

Her uncle had been engaged once, Donna had heard, but his fiancé died of rheumatic fever. She wondered if he would have been more fun-loving if the woman had lived. Probably not. Her uncle was too austere to come between her and her father, Donna decided.

The shadows were lengthening as Nathan's car pulled into the long driveway which led to her grandparents homestead.

Donna's eyes widened.

At the foot of the driveway was the goldfish pond where she and Bill had spent countless hours. Near it was a fenced-in garden, the perfect rows exhibiting her grandmother's painstaking care. There in the yard was the climbing tree where she had acquired many unheeded scraped knees and elbows. The corners of the front lawn were bordered with bright orange tiger lilies. On the other side of the yard were the tall stalks of pink and purple larkspur, which her grandmother had planted to spell out her name many years ago. Past the yard was the orchard with its countless apple, pear, and cherry trees. Beyond the orchard, Donna remembered very well, was the barn and fields where her grandfather spent his days.

But there in the center of the well-kept yard was the two-story white farmhouse, its three gables pointing skyward. Across the front of the house stretched the covered porch. And there she saw her grandparents standing, all smiles, waving to her as the car pulled up. Between them stood a small boy.

Donna called a hasty farewell to Uncle Nathan as she scrambled out of the car. With outstretched arms her grandmother was making her way toward her.

"Hello, Donna, and welcome back home. We've been waiting for you all day. Haven't we Dick?"

Donna rushed into her grandmother's arms. Her grandfather came next, wearing the old overalls she always remembered "Wonder how many pairs he has?" she thought as she hugged him. Then she turned toward the little boy and reached out her hands. "Hi Dick," she said looking into the eyes of her little brother. She still thought of him as a toddler, but the toddler was gone. His brown eyes widened as he looked at the sister he had heard so much about.

"Hi Donna," he said quietly, "I'm glad you could come and

see me."

"I'm so glad I get to see you too, Dick."

The little boy's eyes lit up "Do you want to see the new kittens in the barn?"

Donna looked to her grandmother. "You two go see those kittens," she laughed. "But I'll have dinner ready soon."

Hand in hand, Donna let Dick lead her across the yard, through the orchard and to the barn, though she could have closed her eyes and gone there herself. Once this farm had been home to her, she reflected. Now, a brother she barely knew was showing her around as though she were a guest.

Dick took her to the corner of the barn. There was the litter of five kittens, just opening their eyes. Then her brother showed her the new heifers and the baby chicks that were already half grown. Dick proudly introduced her to the new farm dog.

Donna knelt to pet the dog and heard another voice call her name. She looked up to see Aunt Verna approaching, a smile on her face. Donna stood, somewhat unsure of what to expect from her aunt.

"Well, Donna, here you are. Let me see you. Stand up now. Yes, you have grown haven't you?"

Donna always remembered Verna as a strict, old-maid. It was Verna, not her parents or grandparents, who had always disciplined Donna when she was young. It was Verna who had made her write, "I will always tell the truth," one hundred times when a childish lie had punctuated her stories. Even now, after having been gone for several years, Donna wondered if Aunt Verna was going to punish her for some misdeed that was discovered after her departure. But Verna apparently was not considering any disciplinary matters at the moment.

"I see Dick has been introducing you to the new animals on the farm. He's been quite eager to see his big sister from the East, haven't you Dick? Well, let's head back to the house and we can all hear about your school and friends in Massachusetts."

As the threesome made their way back toward the farm house, Donna wondered if she should mention her plan to stay in Kansas. Aunt Verna always had an opinion about everything. Would she be in favor of Donna returning to Kansas? Or would she want Donna to return to her father, who was Verna's brother? Donna decided it was better to say nothing than risk Verna taking the opposite side of the argument.

Back at the farmhouse, Donna recognized an old pick up. "Uncle Boyd," she exclaimed. Mindful of Aunt Verna's presence, she checked the urge to dash into the house. But before she reached the house, the screen door opened and her uncle came out laughing.

"Hey there, how's my favorite niece," Uncle Boyd called to her. It was a joke between them. She was his only niece.

"I didn't know you were going to be here, Uncle Boyd," Donna responded, rushing up to the back porch.

Aunt Marge joined them on the porch. "When he heard you were coming home, he insisted we drive down from Topeka this very night," she stated. "He even took off from work early. And he never does that."

Donna's face beamed as the group made their way into the farmhouse kitchen. She inhaled the aromas coming from the old fashioned cast iron stove and noted the platters of heaping food. Grandma never found it difficult to cook for a crowd.

"Looks like Bob and Margaret are here as well," Verna informed them glancing out the window. Bob was her father's youngest brother who lived with his wife across the road from Grandma and Grandpa and helped them farm the homestead.

It was a happy, noisy group that gathered around the table.

A moment of quiet was heard while her grandfather said grace, giving thanks for Donna's safe arrival and the presence of three of his four children at the table Immediately following, the clatter of dishes and laughing filled the dining room.

Donna enjoyed the happy bantering of Uncle Boyd and Uncle Bob teasing each other. Aunt Margaret and Aunt Marge joined in.

"So tell us about your school," Verna prompted. Aunt Verna had been a school teacher when she was younger. During the war, she had felt it her duty to become a nurse to help care for the country's wounded. Now, she had put her two careers together as a school nurse. But she never seemed to lose her interest in teaching. "A typical old-maid school marm," many people, including Donna, had whispered behind her back.

"I will be starting high school this year," Donna began. "It's a separate school from the junior high where I have been."

"And your stepmother teaches in the high school?" Uncle Boyd asked.

"Marion? Oh no. She teaches third grade."

"So you never had her as your teacher, I take it," her uncle quizzed.

"No," Donna exclaimed. "I moved to Massachusetts when I was in the seventh grade. I never went to the elementary school where Marion teaches."

"And it would be most inappropriate for a student to have a parent – even a stepmother – for a teacher," Aunt Verna chimed in. "Sometimes it can't be helped in some smaller districts, but it's never a good situation, I've always said. And," she added, "I'm surprised your stepmother allows you to call her by her first name."

"Oh, I always have," responded Donna. "That's how she introduced herself to me. I mean, it wouldn't seem natural to

73

call her 'Mother', seeing how I already have a mother."

The room became quiet for a moment. Donna was aware of the clock ticking and the sound of silverware scraping the china plates.

"Well," said Aunt Verna after a lengthy pause, "I'm not sure how much Marion and I would agree on certain issues."

Donna saw her uncles exchange glances and suppress their grins. Verna saw it too.

"A teacher should have utmost character if she is to be an example to her students," Verna stated. It sounded as if she was getting started on a lesson herself.

"Oh admit it," Bob said good-naturedly. "You don't like anyone who would take one of your brothers so far away."

"It started before that," Boyd retorted quickly. Donna looked at her uncles, hoping they would explain Aunt Margaret and Aunt Marge looked down at table.

"I have three perfect brothers," Aunt Verna replied pointedly. "It just so happens that one of them has not had good judgment in choosing women of character."

Donna was aware that the others had glanced her way. But it was Boyd who spoke up. "There's no reason to bring all that up, Verna," he stated quietly. "Donna is here on a holiday, and a holiday we are going to make it."

"And we are all very glad you are here," her grandmother responded.

"Yeah," Dick put in It was the first time he had spoken since the meal began, "because Grandma made chocolate cake."

Everyone laughed. Donna slowly released her breath as a new conversation started between Bob and Boyd. Her fork pushed the food around on her plate, her appetite diminished. "It's not just Marion that Verna was talking about" she thought. "She was also talking about my mother. But why?"

Dinner over, the family made their way into the parlor. It wasn't long before the conversation centered on farming and the current price of corn. Donna half listened. She had almost forgotten that this was a perpetually favorite topic of discussion, whether she spent the evening with Cora and Nathan or Grandma and Grandpa Hogue. She couldn't remember ever hearing Marion or Kithy discuss the cost of crops. A smile cut across her face as she thought of their reaction if she tried to bring the subject up. But here in Kansas? "Almost like living in a different country," she mused.

Her eyes made her way around her grandmother's sitting room. Like Aunt Cora's parlor, it was comfortable and homey, not like their formal living room back East. But still, it was different from Cora and Nathan's home. She tried to put her finger on the difference.

"But does corn bring a higher price in East Kansas than in West Kansas?" Boyd was asking.

The gong of the mantle clock drew her attention. Marion had a large grandfather clock, an antique that had been in the family for a long time. It was an all-wooden clock and one of her stepmother's most prized possessions. Grandpa Hogue's clock was petite with a painted brass face. Cora, of course, didn't have such any such clock.

"It's money," Donna realized with a sudden recognition. The Hogue farm was far more prosperous than Nathan's. She never realized it before, but it suddenly was obvious. The large acreage and two tractors of her grandfather reflected a bountiful farm. Grandpa Hogue even owned a thrasher, one of the few farmers in the county that had one. The rugs and furniture, even the well laden table indicated a more affluent life-style than the austerity of Cora and Nathan's simple home.

"My mother comes from a poorer family, I guess. Is that

what Verna was indicating about her father's choice of women?" Donna wondered.

No, Marion's father had come from a prosperous family, so it couldn't be related to wealth. Or could it?" Donna pondered.

She closed her eyes, trying to tune out the sounds of the discussion around her. Instead she heard her grandmother's rocking chair and the crickets chirping in the fields. They were comforting sounds that seemed to ease the disquiet in her soul. She slipped outside onto the front porch and stood still listening.

It wasn't long before her grandmother stood beside her. "Anything wrong, Donna?" she asked.

"No. I was just remembering how the cornstalks talked?"

"Cornstalks talked?" her grandmother tilted her head towards her.

"When we would sit on the porch in the evening we could hear the creaking sound of the cornstalks growing. I used to imagine that the cornstalks on one side of the field were talking to those on the other."

Her grandmother laughed. "Children do have such an imagination. But, yet, it is really true if you are quiet you can hear the cornstalks rustling as they actually grow. Shhhh. Listen."

They both stood silent, side by side listening. Donna could hear a car pass on the road and a dog bark from a distant farmhouse.

There it was. A creaking sound came from the fields. She looked at her grandmother and they both laughed.

"Knee high by fourth of July," they both quoted together.

"Well the fourth of July isn't quite here and the cornstalks reach well past my knees," Donna said. "So it looks like it will be a good crop this year."

"Yes, it looks good," her grandmother agreed. "The last few years have been very good."

"Tired of our conversation about crops, Donna?" asked Uncle Bob as he stepped out onto the porch and joined them.

"No, as a matter of fact," his niece replied, "Grandma and I were just talking about the corn out here."

"It's a beautiful sight," her uncle replied, looking across the fields. "Boyd moved to Topeka and your father moved to Massachusetts. But not me. I'll take the farm over the city any day."

"That's how Bill feels," Donna responded, wishing she could have seen her brother here at his own home.

"Yes he does, he has it in his blood," Uncle Bob agreed. "When the explorers first came to this land they were looking for the proverbial cities of gold. Well here they are," he said, pointing to the fields. "Golden fields of corn and wheat, clean air, and a golden sunrise every morning. City life with its traffic and smoke just doesn't cut it."

"Speaking of cutting," said her grandmother, "how about we go in and cut the cake your little brother has been waiting for all day? We also have some hand-cranked ice cream he doesn't know about."

"Made with cream from your Jersey cows?" Donna asked.

"You know it," her grandmother answered. As they turned toward the farmhouse door, her grandmother tousled her hair. "It's sure good to have you home, Daughter."

"It's good to be home, Grandma," Donna whispered. With crickets chirping, the glow of kerosene lamps inside the farmhouse, and surrounded by the loved ones she had known her whole life, she felt like she was home.

So why did she feel so alone, as if she didn't quite belong?

7

A Saturday in Eskridge

Donna woke to the sound of birds chirping and insects humming. Sunlight gleamed through the organdy curtains as they fluttered in a soft, morning breeze. She inhaled the delicious aroma of sausage and biscuits. Still, she didn't rush to get out of bed.

Conversations from last night kept running through her head. What did Aunt Verna mean by saying her father did not have good judgment in choosing women of character? That she was referring to her mother seemed obvious. Was she also referring to Marion?

Donna reflected on how Marion's friendliness always turned to cold silence when she mentioned her mother Hazel. Had Hazel somehow offended Marion or Aunt Verna? That didn't seem likely. Her mother was the least opinionated of the three and seemed the least likely to give offense or take offense. Her own mother had scolded Donna less than her aunt or stepmother.

When Aunt Cora and Uncle Nathan had picked her up last night, she had tried to approach the subject with them. "Did my mother and Aunt Verna get along?" she had asked.

"I don't remember the two of them ever arguing," Cora had stated before changing the subject. What else could she have expected? Cora never gossiped.

Lying in bed, Donna heard Old Blue neighing in the barn. Suddenly, she remembered Tony. With a quick motion she threw back the covers and felt for her slippers on the hard floor. It took little time for her to get washed up for the day and dressed.

She found her uncle already in the barn. "Morning," he called to her.

"How's Tony doing, Uncle Nathan?"

"Oh, don't know that one night has made a lot of difference one way or the other."

"Can I ride him now," Donna asked as she ran her hand through his dark mane. "I mean, do you think he's well enough for me to ride him?"

"Don't think there's much more you could do that he'd like better," her uncle answered. "Don't need to race him or anything. Just a little trot down the lane and back might really pick up his appetite."

"Thanks, Uncle Nathan. I won't go too far or too fast," she replied. It took no time to get her pony saddled and headed toward the road.

It was a quiet morning. The pony plodded down the unpaved country road with no traffic to disturb their pleasant venture. Rounding a corner, Donna found herself eye to eye with another creature. It was a doe. Donna caught her breath and stared in wonder at the sand-colored animal. For a moment she and the doe locked eyes. Then it turned and fled into some nearby bushes.

"Did you see the deer?" the girl murmured to her pony. "I haven't seen one for years. Actually", she added, "since I left Kansas. I guess it makes sense there are more out here than back East."

The girl and pony continued their leisurely morning trek.

But the painfully beautiful eyes of the doe haunted her. The creature seemed almost human in a way, both yearning and nervous at the same time. The eyes reminded her of something. Or was it someone?

A distant sound of screeching tires alerted her to a sole car on the intersecting country road they were approaching. "Come on, Tony, time to turn around and go home." She turned his reins, but Tony needed no urging to turn back toward his stall. Sluggishly, he headed home.

Donna considered urging him into a trot, but thought better of it. She wistfully recollected cantering carefree up and down this road on his back. "You are going to get better, Old Boy, aren't you?" He continued walking. How different her pony was from the deer. Slow and trusting, he had never run from her. With a start she realized who the deer reminded her of.

Her mother.

"That's strange," she thought to herself. Her mother wasn't shy like the deer; but she was beautiful. She shook the thought out of her head and continued her ride back to the farm.

"I'll unsaddle him," her uncle stated as she returned to the barn. "You go ahead and get your breakfast. Your aunt has plans for the morning, I think." Donna willingly handed the reins to her uncle's rough, leathery hands, then sauntered toward the house.

"Good morning, Donna," her aunt greeted her as she entered the kitchen. "Did you and Tony have a nice ride together?"

"We did. We saw a deer at the end of the road."

"Yes, you seem them early. Once the cars get on the road they hide themselves."

"I didn't see many cars," her niece reported.

"We can have a dozen or so cars pass in a day."

Donna suppressed a smile and eyed the breakfast her aunt had saved for her. As Donna devoured the biscuits her aunt remarked, "My stars, Child, that early morning hike in the fresh air certainly gave you an appetite."

"No one makes sausage and biscuits like you, Aunt Cora."

Cora laughed. "I just bake plain old biscuits and fry the sausage like everyone else in the country."

"Well, I haven't been in the country for a while," Donna replied. "I almost forgot what country cooking tastes like."

"Speaking of the country, I'm going to the Grange to pick up some groceries and supplies. Do you want to come along?"

Donna finished her orange juice unhurriedly as she thought of her answer.

"Aunt Cora," Donna began. "I was wondering."

"Yes."

"I mean," she stammered. "I was hoping that maybe I would get to visit with Aunt Pearl."

Cora looked pleased. "I know Pearl would be happy to see you. Perhaps we can stop in together after we go to town."

Donna tried to be tactful. "I mean, would it be okay if I visited with Pearl while you went to the Grange without me?"

Cora seemed nonplussed. Then she chuckled. "I don't see why not. I'm sure our little Grange store is nothing compared to the stores you shop at in Boston. And Pearl was asking about you last week. I'm sure she would be right glad to have a visit with you. I'll just ring her up and make sure she's going to be home."

Cora turned to the wall phone and began to turn the crank. Donna heard her ask the operator to connect her to Pearl.

The last thing Donna wanted to do was deceive Aunt Cora.

But she was quite content to let her aunt assume the small Grange where eggs, milk, and cream were exchanged by farmers was of no interest to her. Instead, her mind churned as she tried to picture Aunt Pearl.

Would Pearl be an effective ally? Aunt Cora was unlikely to interfere with her father's plans. But Aunt Pearl? There was only one way to find out, she concluded as she swallowed the last biscuit.

Later in the morning, Donna and Cora pulled into the driveway of a quaint farm house. There was Aunt Pearl at the doorway waving to her. Donna got out of the car and called a hasty farewell to Cora.

"I'll be back after I've done my errands," Cora called as the car pulled out of the driveway.

"Well, Donna," Aunt Pearl greeted her with a hug. "I was so hoping we would have a chance to visit when I heard you were coming to Kansas for part of the summer. Then Cora called this morning and said you were coming by. So good to see you."

"It's good to see you too, Aunt Pearl."

"Don't mind helping me in the kitchen, while we visit, do you?" her aunt asked.

"Not at all," Donna responded.

She entered the kitchen and breathed deeply. Aunt Pearl's farmhouse was as quaint as Aunt Cora's. The white clapboard house with its red brick chimney and porch stretched across the front was surrounded by a neat green lawn and colorful flower beds. Inside, the old fashioned furniture and portraits blended with the more modern crank telephone and ice box.

"Why don't we shell some peas together, shall we?" her aunt mentioned. "We can take these out on the porch and sit in the shade and talk."

They both carried the pans out to the porch. The two sat side by side on the red porch swing, each with a bowl of peas in their lap and the large pot between.

"Now," said her aunt getting settled. "Why don't you just tell me about life in Massachusetts?"

"I go to a big school," Donna began with enthusiasm. "And we live near the Atlantic Ocean. Kithy loves the ocean – she's my stepmother's mother. And my father has a square dance barn and we have square dances every Saturday night."

Words tumbled out of Donna's mouth. Neither the creaking of the old swing or the calm face of her aunt whose work-worn hands deftly spilled the contents of the shelled peas hindered her speech.

Pearl just rocked and listened. No interruptions indicated anything about Donna's life in Massachusetts might offend her listener. A few moment of silence followed Donna's recital of the most interesting aspects of her life. She took a breath.

"Aunt Pearl, I do have a question for you."

"What is it, Child?"

"Um, it's about our family," Donna stammered.

"Out with it. I'll answer it if I can."

"I heard, well, I mean my father, he said that Aunt Cora is actually my grandmother." Donna saw Aunt Pearl's eyes arch. "That's what he told me, or at least he said that's what he and lots of people think," she continued quickly.

Pearl set her bowl down and turned to her younger visitor.

"Well, Donna. I can see you have some real questions. You've grown up. You're not a little girl anymore, and I guess it's time we had a heart to heart talk."

"To begin with, you need to know that Cora is not your grandmother. She never had any children of her own – though she certainly helped raise a lot of them."

"But my father…" Dona began.

"Your father is no expert on the matter," her aunt cut in, a little sharp rise to her voice. "He was a baby at the time your mother was born and wouldn't have known one way or the other. I, on the other hand, probably know Cora better than anyone else. She, of course, is your aunt; and I am actually her aunt. But we really are more like sisters; because we are the same age and were born on the same day of the same year."

"I've always wondered about that," Donna quipped.

Aunt Pearl grinned. "You aren't the first one to wonder. You see my mother's name was Catherine, Catherine Dehart Cloud to be exact. Catherine had two daughters. I am her youngest daughter but her oldest daughter is my sister Mattie who was 21 years older than I. My sister's full name was Sarah Martha Cloud, though everyone called her Mattie. By the time I was born she had married Ed Grimm and lived not far from us.

"Now the funny thing was that even though Catherine and Mattie were mother and daughter, it just so happened that they both gave birth to baby girls on the same day. Those girls are none other than Cora and I. So even though Cora is actually my niece, she was almost like a twin sister to me. We have been very close all of our lives.

"My sister Mattie was a stern woman. She died a few months after you were born so of course you wouldn't remember her. Cora never complained about her mother, but she was always quite strict with Cora. Mattie seemed to leave much of the care of her other children to Cora who was her oldest.

"After Cora graduated from high school she went to college in Manhattan. I think Mattie realized then how much she depended on her daughter, because after two years Cora returned back to the farm.

"Then when Cora was planning on getting married, her

84

mother stepped in and interfered. Lots of us were perturbed at Mattie. Cora never married after that and never had another beau."

Donna had been listening carefully. "I didn't know Aunt Cora was ever engaged," she interrupted.

"I expect she hasn't said much about it lately. But believe me, she and I discussed that and quite a few other matters over the years."

"But I'm getting a little ahead of myself," her aunt back tracked. "When her four boys were getting a bit older, Mattie decided she wanted another little girl and they filled out some paperwork to that end. Well, one day our country doctor came and told Mattie that there was a baby girl who was sick and wasn't expected to live. That baby was your mother, and as you know she didn't die. The boys wanted to keep her, and so the family adopted her and gave her the name Hazel Grimm.

"By this time Aunt Cora was a young woman. So when a baby showed up at the house, people started making assumptions. But believe me, I of all people, would have known if Cora had been pregnant.

"Your mother was a few years old when Cora got engaged. Personally, I don't think Mattie liked the idea of Cora moving away from home when there was still a little one in the house. So one day Nathan told his mother that he had seen Cora's fiancé talking to another woman in town. That was the reason Mattie needed. She told Cora that her beau was unfaithful and demanded the engagement be broken off.

"So Cora never married and she never left the farm again. Nathan's story is similar. He had been engaged but his fiancé had died. One by one the other brothers married and moved away, but Cora continued as the housewife at the farm – although she wasn't a wife. With time, her parents died and she and Nathan continued at the farm – he in the fields and she keeping house as she always had.

"Meanwhile, your mother was growing up. When she was young, the family wrote to the Kansas Children's Home and asked to see if they could find anything about Hazel's history. All anyone could tell them was that she was born in a camp for homeless people in Dodge City. Court records showed her birth date and her mother's name, but that was about all.

"Once Hazel had grown, she started looking for her mother herself. She didn't find her mother but she found something else a bit interesting," her aunt added. "She had been taken in by another family – name of Matthews I think – who planned to adopt her. But they gave her back to the state. No record of why they gave her back, but considering your mother's condition I've wondered if it might be because she was so sickly. I've also wondered if she was sickly because they hadn't cared for her. We'll never know, I guess.

"Your mother tried to find information about this other family who had taken her for adoption to see if they could help lead her to her biological mother. In the file was a letter Mrs. Matthews had written asking to get the baby back. But by then she was already taken in by Mattie and her husband. After that, the Matthews apparently moved to Oklahoma. Your mother has not been able to locate them or her real mother.

"Meanwhile, back here in Eskridge, no one knew where Hazel had come from. Some thought Cora might be her mother. Cora was old enough for sure. Cora had been engaged and the engagement was broken off. Cora never got married, and Cora was the one that did all the work raising the child. That's mighty fertile ground for those who are prone to assumptions and gossip."

"It's horrible what people say," Donna injected.

"What do you mean?"

"I've had people talk about me because my parents are divorced. And people have said bad things about my mother to my face. You just don't know what it's like."

Aunt Pearl guffawed. "I don't know what it's like? Do you know much about what I've been through or what people have said about my family?"

"No," her great-niece replied. "What?"

"Well, Child, let me tell you. Maybe you have heard and maybe you haven't. When I was raising my four kids my husband got sick. His behavior became erratic and we had to put him in a mental hospital.

"Yes, we did," her aunt continued as she saw Donna's questioning eyes. "It was hard enough having him gone and the kids missing him. Hard to put food on the table and pay the bills. But then there was talk. Oh, did people talk.

"It's one thing to make me feel bad, but when you hurt a child you hurt the mama even more There my kids were struggling day in and day out. And people talking and ostracizing them."

Pearl looked off in the distance. The squeak of the swing was the only sound that was heard.

"I feel bad that happened to you," Donna said finally. "I don't know why people are so horrible."

"Well, I guess I've learned the answer to that," Aunt Pearl stated, her eyes focusing on Donna again and her face more relaxed.

"Why?"

"Something different comes along and they try to make sense of it. They are just trying to get their own world in order and they talk to help themselves sort it out. Folks don't necessarily mean any harm in all their talking – just is their own way of coping with life's ups and downs."

"But it hurts others," Donna argued.

"That is does, Young Lady. That it does. And you know what you need to do when that happens?"

"What?"

"You have to forgive them," the older woman answered. "You have to dig down deep and find the goodness to let it go and think no harm of the gossipers."

"But they hurt other people," Donna reflected.

"Yes. And I found it was harder to forgive those who accidentally hurt you. It's one thing to forgive someone who did something wrong and then feels bad about it. And it's possible to forgive even if they don't feel bad about it. But it's so much harder when someone does you wrong when they weren't trying to, and they never even paid enough mind to know that's what they've done."

"So why do you have to forgive them?"

"Because you become old and bitter if you don't. Doesn't hurt them any; you only hurt yourself when you hold a grudge."

"My dad's not a bitter person," Donna responded. "But he's mad at you. Says you always take my mother's side."

Aunt Pearl laughed. "I told your father to his face that he had not done right by his family and he wasn't particularly keen on hearing it."

"You told my father what?" Donna asked in surprised. She had never seen anyone cross her father before.

"I simply told him what's what," Pearl continued. "He decided to get married and have a family. Then he left you. That's wrong and I told him so."

"He blames my mother."

"Of course he does. They blame each other. Truth is, both

of them are two big kids still wanting to have a good time. So be it. But when you start bringing children into the picture, someone has to take care of them.

"Well your father found another woman, that was your first stepmother – not the woman he's married to now. So he left your family. He can blame Hazel all he wants, but he's the one that left you all.

"But what was worse," her aunt continued, "he wouldn't let you have a stable home. Pulling you back and forth from one place to the next. He wouldn't let Hazel keep her own children. So I told him, 'It's not right how you are moving those kids all over' I said. 'They need a real home. If you aren't going to give them a decent home, then let them stay with their mother and we will help her out best we can.' "

"What did he do," Donna inquired.

"Well, did he let your mother keep you?"

"No. I've never lived with her since I was small," Donna answered.

"Did he let you stay with Cora?"

"For a while," Donna replied. "I've always loved being with Aunt Cora."

"She's a good one, she is. A real saint if I ever met one. But just the time you and Bill would get settled, along comes your father with some other plan. Then his cousin Evert Hogue wanted to adopt you."

"I remember," said Donna suddenly. "Uncle Evert I called him. He and his wife used to come over and take me places with them. But," she added slowly, "I haven't seen them in years."

"That's right, you haven't. Your father not only wouldn't let Evert adopt you, but he wouldn't let you see them again either. After that, I got a bit perturbed and had a talk with your father myself. And apparently," Pearl added with a chuckle, "he still hasn't forgotten it."

"No, he hasn't," Donna answered thoughtfully. "And that explains a few things. Like Daddy saying you always took my mother's side."

"Oh, I can't say I've always taken your mother's side on everything," Pearl replied. "But, with Hazel, well there is a different story there."

"What do you mean?"

"Some people think babies don't know much about what goes on around them; but I disagree. She went from home to home in her first months of life. Then when she was adopted her adopted mother didn't do much of the nurturing herself Deep down inside, I think that can affect a person. I think your mother has always been looking for someone to care about her. Maybe she's looking for her real mother. Maybe she doesn't think the rest of us care enough."

Donna thought again of the deer she had seen that morning "Aunt Pearl, what do you think my mother is looking for?"

Aunt Pearl was quiet a moment before she responded. "Your mother," she said quietly, "has been so obsessed with finding her own mother; she never noticed her children were looking for her."

The young girl and older woman sat side by side in silence for a few minutes. Donna reflected on the years she had spent moving, going from school to school. She would get settled in one place, only to find she was moving again. Whether she knew it or not, Aunt Pearl had answered questions not only about her mother's childhood, but also her own.

The sound of crunching gravel was heard. From the corner of her eye she saw Cora's car coming down the lane. Pearl turned her head and also saw the car approaching.

"Well now, it looks like Cora has finished her errands. I don't know if she thought we would get into all of this. But you did have some questions on your mind. And I hope we will have another chance to visit before you go back to Massachusetts."

"So do I," Donna answered as she hugged her aunt goodbye. With a wave she trotted toward the Chevrolet. "But just maybe," Donna said to herself as a new plan was forming in her head, "things will be different."

Chapter

Tony

The week passed quickly as Donna readjusted to the routine of farm life. She particularly liked milking time when Nathan's Holstein cows trudged noisily to the barn with their low moans. She knew her grandparent's Jersey cows were more profitable, with their richer milk and greater volume of cream. But she liked Nathan's black and white Holsteins better anyway, with their friendly looks and distinct markings. Side by side with Uncle Nathan she poured the milk into the separator and watched the thick lush profitable cream divide from the thinner milk, both of which her aunt would sell at the Grange.

Of course she found time every day to read. Country or city, Donna loved reading. Cora enjoyed good books too, her niece knew, though farm life left relatively little time for her to satisfy that pleasure. Though at a drop of a hat Cora would go on a walk with Donna to discuss what she was reading.

Several times a day Donna and Tony would go out together. "A dog may be a man's best friend," she told him as she brushed his coat, "but you are mine." With Donna's daily attention, he seemed to be getting more lively. "Maybe he is happy I am here," she speculated.

But her fourth day back in Kansas, things changed. When she arrived in the stable in the morning, Tony did not rise when she approached him. Alarmed, she opened the creaking gate and slipped into his stall. Kneeling by his side in the dim

92

light, she noted he was breathing heavily. He lifted his head briefly and neighed as she stroked his mane. Yes, he knew she was there.

"Nathan," she called. "Uncle Nathan!"

When she didn't get an answer Donna stood up. "I'll be back, Tony. I'm going to get Uncle Nathan."

She dashed from the stable into the bright light of the morning sun as Nathan's pick-up truck pulled up to the barn.

"Uncle Nathan," she was at the side of the truck before he got out. "Tony is not well."

"Yes, I noticed he wasn't up and had no interest in his oats this morning," her uncle answered. "Was just coming back from the field to check on him now."

The two entered his stall together. Nathan looked down at the animal.

"He just doesn't look right. Was hoping he'd get better, but seems he has taken a turn for the worse."

"Oh Uncle Nathan! Isn't there anything you can do? I mean, can you get medicine or something?"

"I'm not a veterinarian, though at times like these I wish I was. Did you ask your grandfather about him the other night?"

"My grandfather? Oh Uncle Nathan, I forgot to ask him. I meant to. But Uncle Boyd and Uncle Bob were both there, and of course Aunt Verna, and well, I'm sorry, I forgot to ask.

But you know what?" she continued. "I know they wouldn't mind if I called and asked Grandpa. Of course he would be in the fields right now. Or we could just go over. Can't we? You will talk to my grandfather won't you?"

"Let me get the morning chores done first," he answered thoughtfully. "You run and tell Cora that after lunch we'll be heading over their way."

She threw her arms around her uncle. "Thank you, Uncle

Nathan. I'm sure Grandpa Hogue will know just what to do."

She ran into the farmhouse and alerted Cora to their plans. Then Donna returned to the barn to wait the long morning hours at Tony's side, her book neglected.

"What is it, Boy? What do you need?" she whispered to him. He lifted her head as she spoke to him. That gave her hope. "My grandpa will know what to do. He's not a vet, but he's just about one. I mean, he's taken care of every kind of farm animal that ever was."

It was close to noon when Nathan returned. Donna didn't stop for lunch and shook her head when Cora suggested it. She climbed into Nathan's truck. The two were quiet on their way over to the Hogue farm.

As the pick-up pulled into the driveway, she saw her grandmother standing at the porch with the gong in her hand. She turned toward the approaching truck, shading her eyes to see what visitors approached. As Donna emerged from the truck her grandmother's face lit up with a smile.

"My stars, Daughter, I wasn't expecting you today, but it sure is good to see you. Come in, come in, we're just getting lunch on the table."

Her grandmother turned to speak to Nathan. After years of transporting kids back and forth, the families had always greeted each other from their vehicles and discussing times of exchange from an open window. Now, the woman wondered as the tall, lanky Nathan emerged from the truck and followed his niece.

"Afternoon, Mrs. Hogue. Don't mean to intrude on you without warning. But Donna's quite concerned about her pony. We thought Mr. Hogue might be able to shed some light on what's ailing him."

"By all means, Nathan. The men will be returning in answer to my call shortly. Would you care to join us for lunch?"

"Oh no," her uncle protested. "Got too much work waiting at the farm," he explained shuffling his feet. Donna was aware of his faded and patched overalls and the condition of his old truck. She wondered if he felt an intruder around her father's relatives. Or was he mindful of the difference in success between his farm and the Hogue's farm?

"Yes, of course," her grandmother replied. "I certainly understand. But I see Harry coming now. I'm sure he would be happy to offer whatever advice he could to help Donna's pony."

Donna greeted her grandfather with a hug then watched as the two farmers shook hands and exchanged the usual greetings. As he heard about Tony's condition, he herded Nathan toward the barn. Donna followed along listening carefully. Her grandfather suspected it was an illness and not old age affecting Tony. He gave Nathan a half-filled bottle of medication he said he had used for one of his horses last year.

"I expect that will be enough," Grandpa Hogue explained to the two of them. I used only half the bottle on a much larger animal, so I'm thinking it should be plenty for your little pony."

He refused Nathan's offer of money. "Bottle wasn't doing me any good sitting in the shed," he explained. "It likely would have gone bad before another horse got sick. Let's hope it will be just what Donna's pony needs."

He read the appreciation in his grand-daughters eyes and relief in her uncles.

"Why don't you come on in for dinner?" he also offered. "You know Mrs. Hogue is always happy for company."

Donna was grateful Nathan declined. "We want to give Tony the medicine right away," she added in addition to Uncle Nathan's polite refusal to share their meal.

Her grandfather chuckled. "Well, don't expect it to work

by supper-time," he reminded her.

Donna stopped at the farmhouse kitchen to tell her grand-mother about the medicine. Her little brother's eyes lit up when she entered the room, but lost their sparkle when he learned she wasn't staying. After explaining Tony's illness to the child, Donna agreed to return the next day for supper.

She waved to the family lined up on the porch as she climbed into Nathan's pick-up. "You do think the medicine will work, don't you?" she quizzed her uncle as the car headed down the dirt and gravel driveway.

"Sure hope so. Can't make any promises, though. But I expect next thing to hiring a horse vet your grandfather has likely given us the best chance your pony could have."

Donna held on to the hopes of his words. As soon as the truck pulled up to their barn she jumped out. "Whoa, slow down," her uncle called after you. "We don't need you injured as well as the pony sick."

Donna stayed by Tony's side as Nathan gave him the med-ication. She stayed by his side as Nathan went about his afternoon chores. Cora brought her an apple for the horse and cookies for Donna. The pony was not interested.

At her aunt's insistence, Donna left the stable and joined them at the dinner table. But as soon as the meal was eaten, Aunt Cora shooed her from the kitchen.

"I'll take care of the dishes. I know you want to go out and see that pony of yours."

Donna gave her aunt a quick "thanks" and dashed to the barn. Tony was no different. His condition did not change much that night, or the next day either Sometimes Donna sat by his side reading. Other times she would leave him to help her uncle, never straying far from the barn.

It was mid-afternoon when Uncle Nathan reminded her

that she had promised to have dinner with her father's family that night. Quickly she got changed from her barn clothes and was ready for the short trip to the Hogue homestead.

It was a smaller group that gathered around the farm kitchen table at her grandparent's house. Uncle Bob and Aunt Marge as well as Uncle Boyd and Aunt Margaret were gone, leaving her grandparents, Aunt Verna, Dick, and Donna to share the meal together. Worriedly, she described how Tony was doing.

"Give it a little more time," her grandfather urged her. "Just like people, animals don't get better in one day. I understand he hasn't been doing a lot of running lately like he used to, so he may have been under the weather here for a while. You can tell how an animal's feeling by the way they run."

Donna thought about the antelope she had seen from the train window the day she arrived in Kansas. She described it to her grandfather who laughed. "Yep, sounds like a head-strong buck that wants the world to know he is in charge."

"At least," her grandmother interjected, "he likes to think he's in charge. I'm sure the conductor of the train wasn't the least bit intimidated."

"I wish I could ride on a train and see the antelope," Dick said.

"Oh Dick, it is a very long trip from Massachusetts to Kansas," his older sister responded "It's fun at first, maybe, but I think you would get very tired of the trip."

The room grew quiet. She saw her grandmother and Aunt Verna glance at each other. "What did I say?" Donna wondered. "It always seems like there's some mystery. But all I said is it's a long trip."

After the dishes were cleared, she saw her grandmother and Aunt nod to each other in agreement. Verna turned to her niece "Donna, I have something in my room I want to show you. Why don't you come along with me?"

Curious, Donna agreed, and followed her aunt up the stairs of the farmhouse to her aunt's old bedroom. The fragrance of cedar and moth balls greeted her as Verna opened a trunk at the foot of the bed. She reached in and pulled out two quilts, one bright and colorful, the other old and dark. Both were placed carefully on the bed.

"Do you know what these are?"

"I've seen them before. Aren't they quilts that were made by Grandpa Hogue's mother?"

"Yes. You are correct. This colorful quilt was made by my father's mother - Ann Brown Hogue was her name. She was your great-grandmother. Do you remember her?"

"Vaguely," Donna answered. She tried hard to grasp a fading memory. "I remember her being in the parlor downstairs when Bill and I came to visit. I was playing beside her when she fell asleep. A little later everyone started coming into the room and asking me questions. That was a long time ago."

Verna smiled and shook her head. "She didn't just fall asleep, Donna. You were the one who was at her side when she died at the age of 84. We didn't tell you then because you were young and we didn't want to frighten you."

"Anyway, this top quilt she made for you. It is yours." She indicated the colorful quilt.

"Mine?"

"Yes," said Verna, a cheerful smile on her face. "I remember her quilting it as though it was yesterday. Your mother was expecting you and we were all hoping for a girl."

A shadow crossed Verna's face as the mention of her mother and memory of happier times brought conflicting memories to her.

"It's a pretty quilt," said Donna, tracing one of the floral squares.

Verna chuckled. "That material was from the dress I wore the first day of school," she said as she glanced where Donna was pointing. "This might look like a hodge-podge of patterns to you, she said, but it is a quilt of memories for me."

She pointed to another square, "The curtains in the kitchen. They've been replaced now. But Grandma Ann lovingly made this quilt for you. Eventually her hands became so arthritic that my mother had to finish quilting it. But it was always intended for you. You can take it back with you to Massachusetts.

She lovingly placed the quilt in her niece's hands. Donna embraced it. How could she explain that such a quilt that was the heart and soul of the Hogue farmstead would be out of place in her New England home? It belonged here in Kansas, just as she did. But Verna did not notice. She was touching the other cloth.

"This tapestry is much older. It was made by Grandma Ann's grandmother in Pennsylvania and brought out West by covered wagon during the Civil War. Look carefully at the pattern." Verna lovingly ran her hand over the black woven cloth. Donna noted the white flowers and trees woven into the charcoal-colored fabric. She looked up and saw Verna looking intently into her eyes.

"This tapestry will also be yours someday, Donna."

"Both will be mine?"

"Yes. The first quilt is a gift she made just for you. But this other one is a remembrance."

"A what?" the younger girl asked, uncertain of her aunt's nostalgic mood.

"A remembrance. It is a reminder of something very important that each generation must pass to the next."

"Then what are we remembering?"

"A very old family story. In fact, it was the reason our family came to this country. Have you ever heard of John Brown?"

"Yes, he was an abolitionist from Kansas before the Civil War," Donna answered.

Verna smiled patiently. Donna recognized the 'schoolmarm look' and wondered where the conversation was leading.

"Not that John Brown, although I'm glad you remember your Kansas history. We had a great-great-great-grandfather from Scotland by the name of John Brown. Do you know about him?"

Donna frowned as she thought back. "I remember Grandpa Hogue talking about an old ancestor of his mother's. I, I think he showed me a picture once. A long time ago, I mean."

Verna turned and rummaged for something from her bureau drawer. An old photograph. She handed it to Donna who looked at the stern couple in the old black and white picture. She looked at her aunt.

Verna answered the unspoken question. Those are your great-grandparents. Ann Brown is the grandmother who made this quilt. Her husband is Zenas Hogue. They were my father's parents."

Donna studied the picture to see if there was any resemblance to her grandfather.

"They're pretty serious looking. She's kind of pretty. He's almost scary."

Verna laughed. "It was a harder life than you young ones are used to," she answered. "But, yes, she was a pretty woman in her day. Zenas? Well, he was a Civil War soldier. They let their beards grow back then. I can't imagine my father with a long beard like that, can you?"

Donna smirked and shook her head. She couldn't imagine her grandmother tolerating any type of beard, long or short.

"They were Scottish farmers," her aunt continued. "Both the Hogues and the Browns came from old respectable families. 'Tide, betide, whatever betide, Haig shall be Haig of Bemersyde,' " Verna murmured softly.

Donna eyes widened as she stared at her aunt. History, ethic, and grammar lessons were as natural to Aunt Verna as farming was to her grandfather. But what did she mean by a string of such incoherent syllables?

"It's an old line, quoted by Sir Walter Scott, but going back centuries before," Verna explained.

"Sounds like gibberish. What does it mean?"

"It means," her aunt answered firmly, "that the Hogues will be true and loyal no matter what happens. The Haigs of Bemersyde they were called because they settled in Bemerysde more than 500 years ago. The name 'Haigs' was changed to "Hogue" in America; but our ancestors were 'Haigs.'"

Donna stared blankly at her aunt. "Haigs, Hogues, Browns...You are starting to lose me."

Verna smiled faintly. "It's not an easy store to tell, or to hear." She reached again into her drawer for a notebook. "In fact, it's one of the saddest and most beautiful stories you will ever hear."

Part 3

Where Seldom Is Heard

Chapter

Priesthill Farm

1685
Scotland

The afternoon sun cast lengthening shadows across the lonely moor. Between the rolling hills a small figure could be seen carefully picking her way through the heather and moss. She walked as quickly as the burden in her arms and the uneven grassy field would allow.

Her eyes were fixed on her destination, a plain and homey cottage several hundred feet in front of her. It was a singular dwelling, with a few unimpressive outbuildings that marked it as a farm. No other sign of human habitation could be seen across the widening hills. It was a quiet location, with only the sounds of wind from the hills and the occasional bleating of sheep breaking the silence.

But inside the cottage, the girl knew, she would find warmth and help for the burden she carried. Nestled in her arms was a small lamb. She had found it nuzzling its mother who had lain still in the tufts of grass, never to move again. The little girl knew without someone to look after it, the lamb would never survive.

As she neared the cottage, a woman appeared at the door to meet her. "There you be, Lassie. I was wondering, where you had been. But what is this? A lamb?"

"Aye," the girl responded, "I found it past the peat bed up yonder. Its mother has died."

105

The woman and child looked into each other's eyes, almost understanding the thoughts of the other. The lamb was motherless as the little girl had once been. Would the woman offer her kind, motherly hand to the lamb as she had done for the child?

"We will need to feed him then, or he'll not live long," the older one answered. "You must get some milk for him now. Set him down there and I will show you how."

The face of the child looked hopefully. "I will. Do you think he will be fine?"

The woman ran her hands over the body of the lamb. "Aye, he seems healthy, though he is a wee one."

"Can he stay here with me? Do you think my father will let me keep him?"

The woman chose her words carefully. "He will let you nurse him 'til he is grown, of this I am sure, Janet. But if he will let you treat him as a moppet, I cannot promise."

The little one named Janet followed the woman as she prepared to feed the milk put aside for the lamb. She copied the gentle motions and soft coos that coaxed the lamb to accept the milk.

From the corner of the room a small cry interrupted the relative quiet of the cottage. The woman crossed to the cradle in the corner and picked up an infant. "I must feed your brother, Lassie. You must feed the lamb yourself."

"Aye, I will Mother. See how he wants to eat? See, he wants to be here with us, don't you think? "

"To be sure," she responded. Settling into the wooden rocker, she began to nurse her son as she watched her step-daughter feeding the lamb.

Both the boy and the lamb would not be nursed for much longer, the woman thought. She was thankful for the rocking chair her husband had made her. With her growing son and a new baby soon to be born she welcomed the chance to sit and rock. There were precious few comforts in their life, but whatever kindnesses her husband could show to her he was quick to do, she reflected.

Janet giggled as the lamb sucked on her fingers. "I think we should name him, do you not?"

"I see no harm in giving him a name."

"Perchance my father will think of a proper name. Will he not be home soon so I can show him the lamb?"

Again the woman chose her words very carefully. She who had once been cheerful and bright, had come to view all of life with a caution that could not confidently predict the future. How did one provide love and security to a child who had already known such loss, when she knew that death and destruction were so close at hand?

"Your father took the pack mule to town. I expect him back not so long from now," she answered out loud while silently praying for his safe return.

"What did father take to town today?" inquired Janet. "Some loads take him longer than others it seems."

"Aye, you speak right," the mother answered, "depending on who he is carrier for and what his load may be, the trip can be longer or shorter. But for truth, I do not know who he carries for today."

"But why, Mother? Why is it so secret? My father is a carrier, everyone knows that. And he carries vegetables and such common things. I have seen his loads. And yet seldom will you hear who he carries for?"

"Oh my dear child, these are such hard times for our people. Many have been arrested and jailed for nothing. The less that is said about one's business, the less chance that spies or soldiers will hear."

"Does anyone care what he carries on the back of our mule?"

"Nay, it is not the load that is contraband. It is the carrier. Your father himself is a wanted man. His name is on the Royal Proclamation as a fugitive from the law. But everyone in all the area around here knows he is a good, honest servant of God, so they trust him above all others to take their loads to town. But since he does not wish his customers to be harassed for hiring him to carry their goods, he tells not whose goods he carries."

"Is it because he is a Covenanter that he is wanted?"

"Aye, that alone is his crime. And mine too. And all who meet secretly with us here on the moor to pray and worship God. We hold to the covenant, signed by the King of England himself that says the people of Scotland may worship freely. But the current king has burned that covenant and declares that he alone can decide how and where we will worship."

"At our last conventicle Agnes told me that her father and uncle had argued quite harshly," Janet informed her stepmother. "Her uncle says that my father and her father are fools. That all we have to do is accept the Indulgence and we can be free." She looked up at her stepmother. "Can we accept the Indulgence?"

A dark look stole across the kindly face. "No Janet, you must never say that. It is an evil thing."

"Agnes said all we have to do is to go to the church in the town but once in a while. Is it such a sin to go to their church?"

"No, it is not a sin to go to their church. But to accept the Indulgence is unconscionable."

"But what is the Indulgence?"

"It is a black and evil law. It says that we will be forgiven for our crimes of worship if we but accept the compromising ministers their bishops have set in the churches, and state that the king is ruler of all – the state, the church, and our very souls."

"But he is our ruler some say, and we must obey him like any other ruler."

"He is king of the affairs of government, yes. But he goes far beyond that. He is not king of the church. He is not the king who rules our homes and our hearts. Christ alone is King of Kings and Lord of Lords."

"The uncle of Agnes said we are being stubborn Scotts, ready to force our country into civil war rather than to obey a simple law."

"Look at me, Child. This is something you must understand." The daughter stepped closer to look intently at her step-mother, the little lamb forgotten. "We cannot and must not obey a king who is a black-hearted tyrant," continued the woman earnestly. "He says we must obey the law, but he burns the law and declares himself to be above all laws. He says we are law breakers, and sends soldiers to reprimand us by burning our farms and dragging our husbands and fathers to jail with many a beating and on no just charges of wrong doing. He says we must worship in his church, and puts corrupt ministers into the pulpits who preach not God's word but use their position to spy on the very people they are supposed to minister to. No, Janet, we will not stoop to deny the Lord we love in order to pay homage to a tyrant who..."

A muffled sound outside stopped her mid-sentence. Holding her son close she crossed to the window and looked out. For a long moment she said nothing. The little girl watched every movement of her tense body.

She tried to comprehend her mother's behavior. Frequently people came to their cottage by day and by night. Usually they sought help, and never were they turned away whoever they were. Often they stayed for supper, or even spent the night in their home or in the barn. Once a week, on the Sabbath, dozens of people would come to their home to hear her father teach the Scriptures. They came quietly, one by one, and guards were always posted.

And sometimes – and this was the most exciting of all – a conventicle would be held near their home. These were the most joyous occasions, when hundreds and sometimes even thousands of people would gather to hear one of their preachers preach. She knew her father helped organize the conventicles, but they were always held in different places so the authorities would not catch them. Often the Covenanters would come to her father to help prepare the conventicles, even when they were not held on their very own moor.

Her father was a delegate for the United Societies of Presbyterians, she knew. Often the leaders met or sought shelter in their home. Yes, Janet was used to lots of coming and going across the silent moors to their solitary cottage.

But lately her mother had become jittery when she heard the sounds of someone approaching. Everyone would get quiet and start looking around the room, giving her orders and making plans before they even knew who it was that was coming.

Recently, Janet herself had given the alarm that someone was coming. That time two soldiers had come to the door, but not before her father had escaped out the back and over the hills. Janet remembered her step-mother's brave answers that her father was not home, and no, she did not know where he was. And they did not know either. But it had been a long night for them. Her father had returned the next day. He told them he had sought shelter in a cave. To his delight, he found a few other persecuted brethren hiding in the same place. They had spent the night in prayer and psalm singing. It was an elated but tired father who had returned the next morning. He had enjoyed fellowship with like-minded believers all through the night. His wife and child, unfortunately, had not found the hours of separation so blessed.

Now the girl watched as her mother scanned the horizon. "Praise be to God" she said at last. "It is your father. Safely returned home to us again. And he is alone too."

Janet jumped up, and ran to the door and threw it open. "Father, father," she yelled, running to him.

"There is my sweet g-girl," he called taking her into his arms. And my dearest Isabella," he said, embracing her and the baby together, "Are you all w-well?"

"Yes, Husband, we are quite well. How fared your trip to and from Muirkirk?"

"Good, good. Not a problem a' all." Husband and wife looked at each other and smiled gratefully. It was only a few miles from their home, Priesthill Farm, to the town of Muirkirk in Ayrshire, Scotland. The rugged, wild terrain made his services as a pack carrier valuable as few desired to make the difficult journey.

"Father, I have something to show thee."

"D-do you now? Well help me put this most d-deserving mule into his stall and y-you shall show me." The little girl took hold of the mule's bridle and walked joyfully off with her father. She was used to his stammering speech and his gentle manners.

Isabella smiled watching the two go off together. "Well, young John," she said to the baby. "You and I must go to the kitchen and get the supper on the table while they fetch food for the mule."

Shortly after, they all sat around the table together. Isabella listened to her husband give thanks for the food, the safety of

111

home, and the young lamb that Janet had found. The sound of his voice brought comfort to her.

"You sound happy tonight, John," she said as they began eating.

"Indeed, I am. The p-produce was sold profitably to the delight of its owner. He has paid me well and given me a tip to relieve the suffering of our w-widows."

"Oh, he is a Covenanter then?" Janet exclaimed.

Her father smiled at her. "Nay, he is not, Lass. You see, even our n-neighbors who have compromised on the covenant despise the king and soldiers for their injustice and tyranny. Some b-blame us for threatening civil war, to be sure. But many are glad that we resist their evil tyranny. Even to the point of loss of homes and lives. "

"And so," he said, "we do have friends. Some neighbors are spies, but some think kindly of our cause. It is to us they t-turn when their souls are in need of comfort. So some intentionally pay extra to me to help in the relief of the suffering of those who have been turned from their homes or had their farms burnt."

"There is enough suffering, to be sure. One always fears the next report."

"We mustn't live in fear. That is submitting to a greater tyranny, Isabella."

"I know John, but 'tis so many who are jailed, so many who have been hung."

"I told you the night I asked you to marry me that it was a life of danger and hiding, that I had poor security to offer a sweet woman like yourself."

"Aye, Husband, and not once I have regretted it."

A sound of approaching footsteps was heard on the stone outside their door. Isabella's face turned white while her husband's remained composed.

"Take Baby John and Janet into the back room," he said calmly as he rose and handed the baby to his mother. The footsteps were too close. There was no chance for her husband to escape this time.

Where Danger Lurks

Isabella held tightly to Janet's hand and gripped her son as they made their way to the small bedroom at the back of their home. But before they reached the room, the front door of their house opened. Isabella caught her breath.

It was only a single man who strode into their room. She saw immediately he was not wearing the bright red uniform of a British solider, but a tattered brown cape.

"Pastor Peden," declared her husband. "A surprise to see you. A very b-blessed surprise, indeed."

"My apologies for barging in on you like this," he stated. "I was heading to a conventicle in Dumfries when I heard soldiers on the road. I took a rather long-way around the countryside and thought to seek shelter here." He eyed their table they had just left. "But I do not want to intrude."

"You are most welcome," John assured him. Isabella quickly came forward to greet their guest and add another place at the table. Visitors who had traveled under-cover to their home were not uncommon, but her face had a particularly delighted expression now.

"Isabella," the minister turned to her, "you are looking fair and healthy. May I assume your husband is treating you well?"

"Indeed," she answered, "a fine and caring husband you have given me."

"Aye, I told you that the night I married the two of you.

Three years ago it has been now, has it not?"

Isabella nodded without speaking. She recalled his words to her. "Isabella Marion Weir, you have got a good man," Alexander Peden had told her on that night. "But you will not enjoy him long. Prize his company, and keep linen on hand for his burial sheet, for you will need it when you don't expect it, and it will be a bloody one."

A mysterious man was Reverend Alexander Peden, prophetic and friendly; both cautious and daring at the same time. He had many close escapes himself. It was a bond many of them shared.

"It is I that have reason to be thankful," she heard her husband saying as she hung up their guest's cloak. "In spite of the danger I have brought her into, seldom is heard a word of complaint or discouragement. "

"She is both brave and strong," agreed Pastor Peden as they settled at the plain wooden table.

For the second time that night they held hands and gave heart-felt thanks for the traveling mercies that had been bestowed. Visitors were always welcome, but visits from the traveling preachers were special occasions. This gave them a chance to hear what was happening in the wider world and with the congregations further away.

"Last week I was heading to the Black farm," their pastor informed them. "But the dragoons had been there. They have burnt the house, stolen all the animals, and Andrew has been sent to Bass Rock prison."

"God help us!" Isabella uttered, shuddering at the stories that had been repeated at the inhumane treatment of those imprisoned at Bass Rock.

"He is our help, indeed," their pastor replied. "All the others at the farm have been rescued and are being looked after

But these are dark days."

The minister turned to John. "And I hear that the Sabbath school you are teaching here is doing well. Many travel miles across difficult terrain to attend the classes."

"Aye, since the conventicles are fewer and longer in between, owing to the number of our preachers that have been imprisoned, it is to the Sabbath school that many c-come."

"You would indeed have made a fine preacher yourself, John."

"For that I trained, as you know, Pastor. But for the stammering of my t-tongue, I would not have a congregation have to endure such sermons."

"It is the heart, good man, and solid knowledge that avails a man of God. These you possess while many of the publicly appointed preachers speak eloquently but have neither."

Isabella withdrew to allow the men to talk. It was her husband, she knew, that looked after the needs of their local brethren. She knew that when she married him he had the heart as well as the responsibility of a minister, but made his living as a pack carrier and farmer.

But it all worked together well, she reflected. Their lonely moor provided a secure location for the brethren to gather. His frequent trips on the road as a carrier kept him in touch with all the inhabitants around. It would be a good life, if it weren't for the growing sense of danger. But for tonight they were as secure as they could hope to be.

***

The next morning the family arose early, before the sun. Isabella knew their visitor needed to travel as much as possible under the cover of darkness. The small group gathered again around the table. Together they read John 16. Isabella closed her eyes and listened to her husband read the last verse, "In this world ye shall have tribulation, but be of good cheer, I have overcome the world."

"A thick fog has gathered on the hills that makes traveling dangerous," John warned Reverend Peden. "You must be careful with your steps."

"It may be a blessing, this fog," he answered. "Harder for unfriendly eyes to see me."

"But it is also harder for you to see our enemies until it is too late."

"Aye it is. I will use due caution. Would not want to miss the meeting tonight because of carelessness."

Isabella left them to their farewells and picked her way to the barn to get some hay to make a bed for Janet's lamb. 'Alexander' her daughter had named the lamb, after the honored guest who had spent the night with them. Isabella was crossing the yard, barely able to see in front of her due to the mist. She knew the yard well so it was no danger, but she could not see the departing figure a few feet behind her. But she heard his voice.

"Poor woman; a fearful morning is this; such a dark and misty morning." Then he left across the moor.

Isabella shook off the gloom of his mood. She remembered her husband's words that to give in to fear was to submit to tyranny and lose the joy and peace they held so dear.

"Do you carry today," she asked her husband.

"Aye, that I do. But it is not far. I noted that you are low on peat. Me thinks I will cut some for you before I depart."

"That would be good," she answered. "Though I do believe I have enough peat to burn to make today's meals, we never know when additional visitors may require more. But are you sure you have time?"

117

"It is not even six o'clock yet, I have plenty of time."

With a shovel in hand, he headed for the bog above and the behind the cottage. Isabella went inside to begin making the bread for the day's meals. The crackling fire warmed the cottage from the early morning chill. It was cold she thought, considering it was the first day of May. Instead of the cheerful sound of birds that one might expect on a spring day, the fog shrouded them in a thick blanket of gray silence. Neither of them saw or heard the danger until it was too late.

A Remembrance

"Mother, Mother," Isabella heard Janet called. "A great many horsemen are coming down the hill with father."

Isabella's heart stopped. She covered her face with her hands. "That which I feared is come upon us. O give me grace for this hour."

She picked up her unsuspecting baby boy and carried him outside. Peering through the gray mist, she detected movement of a small group of soldiers. So it was true. The day she had long braced herself for had come. Soldiers surrounded John and led him, hands bound, toward where she stood near the door of their cottage.

Their red uniforms indicated it was British regulars leading him. Behind them was a plain clad farmer, a citizen of Muirkirk. Isabella recognized him. He had been to a few conventicles. A spy who had led their enemies to their very door! He looked down at the ground when she saw him. But she gave him barely a glance as the clattering of hooves announced an officer on horseback towering above all of them.

The officer dismounted his horse and strode toward them. "So this is one of the preachers?" he asked the spy, with a nod towards her husband.

"No, not him," the other answered shaking his head. "He does not preach."

"But I daresay he prays often enough."

"That I do," John answered. "And last I knew there were no

119

laws against prayer."

"Against prayer, no. But against neglecting to attend the services of the church there is. What say you to that?"

No answer was given, nor was there time to answer. "Guard the prisoner," he ordered several of his men. "We will search the house." He pointed to two others who accompanied him into the dwelling.

"Yes, Captain Claverhouse," one of the guards answered, tightening his grip on John.

Claverhouse! Isabella started. John Graham of Claverhouse was the man referred to as Bloody Clavers. He viciously oversaw the persecutions of the Covenanters, encouraging rather than punishing ill behavior of the troops beneath him.

John's eyes met hers. His serene face buoyed her failing confidence. "Now, Isabella, the day has come that I told you would come, when I spake first to you of marrying me." Behind her she felt Janet grasping her skirt and laid her hand on the child's head to comfort her.

How hard it would be to see him led off by such a cruel man as Claverhouse. So many of the community leaders that they might have appealed to for help had already been excommunicated or arrested. But they had trusted God. She would not turn back now.

Often they had heard the reports of the inquisition. Several times John had witnessed it and described it to her. The Covenanters would be threatened with arrest, with loss of homes or livestock, even death. But all might be averted if they would accept the Indulgence and deny the covenant.

Would her John deny the covenant now in order to stay with her and the children? Or would he suffer the loss of all things, knowing she suffered the same loss, but staying true to his conviction? She was sure he would not waver.

"I am willing to part with you," she answered, "for I know

you will never speak what is false."

He held her in his eyes, which then looked tenderly at the baby boy she held and little girl clinging to her. She saw love in his eyes. "That's all I desire," he answered her. "I have nothing more to do but to die." Their betrayer shifted uncomfortably.

"Treason," thundered the voice of Claverhouse exiting the house. "The evidence is here. See what more evidence of treason is needed than this!" In his hands he carried a prayer book and papers with the names of other delegates of their society.

He also had some matches and bullets. Neither was illegal to have, but having already concluded the prisoner was guilty it took little to prove his case.

"Will you take the Oath of Abjuration," asked Claverhouse. "Promising not to take arms against the king or any of his officials, denouncing all covenants that have since been nullified, promising to attend the services of the king's curate, submitting your souls to their instruction, praying for the king as ruler over state and church and promising not to meet or fellowship with any who will not take this oath?"

"That I cannot do," John answered. "Christ alone is head of the church and no earthly king can usurp his authority."

"Treason, armed insurrection, and heresy," thundered Claverhouse. "Say good bye to your wife and children."

John left the guards who held him. He approached his family, and kissed them each gently. "May all purchased and promised blessings be multiplied to you," he said to his children who both reached out to him. He knelt on the ground and began to pray. In a strong clear voice, without stammer or doubt, he poured out his petition to God.

As she always had in the past, Isabella took great comfort in the sound of his voice calling out to their Lord. He did not ask for deliverance. He prayed for his nation. He prayed for protection for his family and neighbors. He prayed for forgiveness for his enemies.

"Stop," yelled Claverhouse as the righteous man's prayer continued. "I gave you permission to say good-bye and pray, not to preach."

"Sir," responded John Brown, "if you call this preaching you know nothing of either praying or preaching."

Again, he returned his eyes toward heaven as he opened his heart earnestly to his Maker. Twice more did his persecutor interrupt him, but never did it shake him from what they both knew would probably be their last prayer together.

At last his words ended. She opened her eyes, saw him kneeling in front of her, and prepared to see them pull him roughly to his feet. She expected him to be dragged to prison, an unfair trial, and likely death. She would visit him, she would try to secure his release, but she had no expectations for success. He accepted that he was going to be taken to his final home. She accepted it also.

"The six of you," Claverhouse ordered, pointing to the line of six soldiers. "Fire!"

Isabella was startled. Kill him now? No trial, no sentence? On the mere pretense that he had a treasonous prayer book in his house and a list of names a man would be killed on his own doorstep in front of his children?

"You heard me! I said 'Fire'" yelled Claverhouse again. For a moment, no one moved.

She looked at the calm, gentle face of her husband. She saw the soldiers' faces as well. They looked at John with awe, some moved to tears by the words they had just heard. None of them aimed their weapons at John. They knew him to be just. Might there not be deliverance yet?

In anger, Claverhouse reached for his the pistol in his own belt. Isabella heard the shots as they were fired. She saw her husband's body fall. She heard Janet scream and her baby reaching toward his fallen father. She could barely breathe. For a few seconds the form on the ground in front of her writhed with a short struggle. Then it was over.

"So, Woman," said Claverhouse turning from the body lying still on the ground to face her, "What do you think of your husband now?"

She looked him in the eye. "I always thought highly of him," she answered. But now I think more highly of him than I ever did before."

His eyes squinted with rage. "It would be justice," he snarled, "to put you down with him."

"If it were permitted," she replied, "I do not doubt but your cruelty would go to that length. But how do you plan to answer for this morning's work?"

"To man, I can be answerable," he replied as he swung himself onto his horse. He looked down at her with a sneer. "But as for your God,"he spit contemptuously, "I will take Him into my own hands."

He turned his horse and cantered away without looking at the wreckage he had left at the farmhouse. The soldiers turned to follow him, ashamed of what they had witnessed. The farmer kept his eyes locked on the ground.

As the troops withdrew, Isabella's resolve crumpled. Collapsing on the ground, she touched the body of the man she had loved as her own gave way to sobs.

"His head, Mother. Look at his head," Janet cried. "Oh, I cannot look."

His head was mangled from the gunshot wounds at close range. Parts of his head had been scattered. That is not how she wanted him. She put the stunned little boy down by his father. Taking off her own kerchief, she gathered the pieces of his head that she could and tried to fit them in place. She tied her bonnet around his head, remembering the words of Alexander

Pender that his burial sheet would be bloody.

How she wished the pastor had not left them this morning. John had comforted many widows and grieving parents and orphaned children; was there to be none to comfort his family in their hour of grief? But no, if Alexander Peden had stayed, he would be dead too, and none would benefit from it.

"We are sad for our dear Father," she said to the weeping Janet. "Aye, we are sorely saddened. But let us not forget in our sorrow that he sorrows not. This is his hour of joy."

"Is he with my Mama then?"

"Yes, Lassie. He is with all those he loved who have gone before him, including your mother and your two brothers. But better than that, he is with the Savior he loved ever so much."

She looked at his broken body and the limbs in their unnatural position. She couldn't carry him into the house. She was too far along in her pregnancy that it was not possible. But gently she straightened his limbs.

"What do we do now, Mother?" his daughter asked. What could they do? They could not move him. They lived so far from others that even the sound of the gunshot would not alert any to their need.

"Let's go into the house," she said, leading the two children into their home. Inside, their tears flowed again. They hugged each other and wept. Then they would feel at peace and sit and wait. Isabella tried to make plans. She tried to think of what they would do. The farm produced little but sheep. Without his money as a pack carrier they could not make it.

For hours they sat and waited. Always they were mindful of the dreadful scene on the other side of the door. She nursed her son to sleep and laid him in his crib, the stillness inside the house only occasionally broken by a sobbing wind that would grip their thatched cottage or tears that escaped mother or daughter.

At last others came. It was Mrs. Stevens who came first. Then her husband; and slowly the word got out. People from the villages around came to pay their respects and render what little help they could to the wife of the Christian carrier of Ayr.

His body was carried into the house and laid out. It was decided that they would bury him in the very place he fell, only a few yards from his cottage. A grave was dug, and the body lovingly placed into its final place.

Great was the indignation and wrath of the community at the account Isabella gave. "So now," cried a neighbor, "Bloody Clavers is constable, captain, judge, jury and executioner in one. For naught but a prayerbook, no less."

"This is a bad work," said another. "To such desperate lengths this devil dares to go that even his troops and traitors cannot abide him No Isabella, I fear Bloody Clavers is dangerous beyond measure and without any conscience. I fear for you."

"For me?" Isabella asked, "Why for me?"

"Aye, it isn't enough to make widows and orphans of the lives of innocent worshipers," declared another. "More of our women and lasses are becoming the victims of torture and execution."

"You have seen much. More than that man with a blood-stained heart would want any to bear witness to. Look how many come to see your good husband and pay their respects."

"He is right," said Mrs. Stevens. "You need to leave Priesthill Farm, Isabella. Sooner rather than later. We don't know if and when that son of Satan might come back."

The fears of her friends were not unfounded, Isabella knew. The edict passed just six months before stated widows and children of Covenanters could be turned out of home. Word reached them that John's nephew had also been arrested. Under torture, he had stated that weapons in an underground house belonged to John Brown. Graham of Claverhouse added armed insurrection to the charges against the deceased man.

No one in official status would question his report Few contemplated whether the statements cried out by a man undergoing torture were actually valid evidence. None considered that the victims of 28 years of merciless persecution might construct underground houses in which to hide themselves when soldiers were arresting and hanging them daily. And why should one be surprised that such a people had armed guards posted at their meetings when dragoons were free to steal, beat, rape, or commit any other crime against them?

Isabella left Priesthill Farm that night. She left the rocking chair and cradle John had made her. Another neighbor agreed to take Janet's lamb. She gathered a few belongings and went to stay a short time with one of the families of the covenant.

Crossing the threshold, she looked around at the farm she would never see again. Only twenty four hours ago she was helping her little girl rescue an orphaned lamb. Now, her own children were orphaned.

Her eyes lingered on the new grave of her husband. How little could she perceive that when her cottage had long crumbled into the ground, his grave would remain a memorial. Generations would visit the humble tribute, the only human edifice in that vast wild moorlands spreading in all directions, to pay respects to the simple Christian carrier of Ayr.

Isabella and her children would flee. There was no place in Scotland where they would be safe. She was not afraid. he would never fear again; but neither would she be rash. She would take them to Ireland, where the bloody, spiteful hand of Claverhouse would never reach them.

She didn't know – she had no way of knowing – that the son in her arms and the son in her womb would go even further than Ireland. They would cross the immeasurable ocean to settle on the shores of a vast and distant continent. Flowing through their veins was the memory that justice is never obtained when free people submit to an oppressor who dares to tell them how to live their lives. Never would they sell their freedom - even under threat of death or loss of home - to bow to such a tyrant.

Part 4

A Discouraging Word

Hazel

1948

Donna brushed Tony's coat as he stood patiently in his stall. She talked gently to him, relieved that he was back on his feet, even if he was yet too feeble for her to ride.

Her mind wandered back to the story Aunt Verna had told her two nights ago. At first she tried to brush it off as irrelevant trivia of events that had happened almost 250 years ago. But the image of the woman and her children watching as her husband was martyred on their farm returned unbidden to her thoughts.

Donna had read the account in the notebook her aunt had given her entitled 'Ancestory of James M. Brown' by Andrew Brown. On the first page was a picture of the stone monument at the grave-site with a short hand-written note from the writer to her great-grandmother, Ann Brown Hogue, and dated July 29, 1902. Her favorite subject was history so Donna looked up the account in other books as well.

She found most of the story as her aunt had told her when she read the history of Scotland's Killing Times, the period from 1680 to 1688. Like John Brown, who was her great-great-great-great-great-great-great-grandfather, more than fifteen thousand Scottish Covenanters were put to death in that era.

More recently, some had refuted the stories as fabrications. The Killing Time hadn't really happened, they said; the accounts were greatly exaggerated. A handful of religiously stubborn Scots had died for unnecessary theological questions when the king and council had offered them a reasonable indulgence.

But the story of John Brown could not be refuted. Too many had come to say farewell to the gentle Christian carrier. They had seen the mutilated body at his own doorstep and offered their condolences to the shocked and grieving widow. Try as some might, no one could reasonably doubt that it had happened.

The historical naysayers had tried another tactic. They took the words of Graham of Claverhouse in his report. A few bullets were reported to be found in Brown's home; so he must have been an armed insurrectionist. How could Claverhouse, later known as the Viscount of Dundee, have done anything less than execute the man on the spot!

But even the man's own words condemned him, Donna thought. After the Killing Time officially ended he tried to excuse himself for the deeds that caused the Scottish people to nickname him "Bloody Clavers" by saying he had only followed the orders of his commanding officer.

Even now, Donna reflected, the Nuremberg Trials in Germany heard the same argument from those who had killed innocent Jews. "We were just following orders. It wasn't our fault if the orders were immoral."

No, like the Nazis, the Viscount of Dundee could not wash his hands by claiming to merely follow orders. Thousands of deaths, untold number of victims tortured, and the countryside rampaged could not be absolved by shrugging one's shoulders and claiming he had done nothing more than his job.

Nor could one justify an on-the-spot execution for "treasonous papers" without an evaluation of such papers by an impartial court. Even Claverhouse's statement, "I caused to shoot him dead which he suffered very unconcernedly," could not excuse him; as though the serenity of the martyr at his death justified the executioner. Surely the children who had witnessed such brutality were not unconcerned. How could modern naysayers defend the brutality such young ones had witnessed?

Donna shook her head. "Why, Tony, why?" she muttered to the pony, unable to comprehend the horror of mankind's behavior. The Nuremberg Trials made it plain she couldn't just dismiss it as an ancient crime that civilization had outgrown. Such crimes committed by humanity made the petty gossip that had plagued her seem unimportant in contrast.

Donna led the pony out of the stable into the bright Kansas sunshine. Uncle Nathan said it would do him good to have a walk in the light but warned her it was too soon to attempt even a short ride. Both the pony and the girl appreciated the fresh air.

Leading Tony by his harness, she wondered if Isabella had been able to take their pack mule when she escaped with her children. The thought of her and her mother running away with Tony crossed her mind. Then she laughed at herself for her one track mind.

"Well, Tony," she confided to the pony, "sometimes I have felt like little Janet must have when both her parents were dead. But mine," she added," didn't die. They just weren't around."

But it must have been worse, so very worse, for poor little Janet. She had lost first her mother, then her father, and then her home; and that after watching a brutal killing. And the baby boy who had become Donna's ancestor; how much would a one year old remember of the traumatic scene that unfolded before him? Did such a disturbing memory follow him as he and his brother crossed the ocean to raise their children on free soil?

The two sons undoubtedly told their children and grand-children of the event that caused them to flee their homeland. It was the granddaughter of the older son who was believed to have made the dark tapestry that Aunt Verna said would one day be hers.

"At least," she sighed, "no one is out to kill us."

Later that afternoon as the lengthening shadows stretched across the farmhouse kitchen, Aunt Cora noticed Donna's un-characteristic somber mood. When Uncle Nathan pushed his chair back after scraping his plate clean, Donna started to rise to clear the table.

"Let's sit for a bit, Donna," her aunt invited her. "Nathan's going to see to the animals. But I dare say we both could use a glass of lemonade. Let those dishes be; they'll wait for us. Never saw a dish any worse just because it had to wait to be washed. Here, put some ice in these glasses and I'll pour the lemonade. I squeezed it fresh while you were with your pony this afternoon."

Donna flashed her aunt a smile. No one else in the whole world would leave a table full of dirty dishes just to talk to her. Donna knew well that Cora wasn't taking a break because she herself was tired.

Minutes later she was seated on the peeling porch swing beside her aunt, holding a tall glass of tangy lemonade. Donna peered across the yard to the barn and her uncle's lanky body striding quickly toward the field. She wondered how she would handle it if soldiers came and arrested him for his beliefs. She briefly recounted to Aunt Cora the story Aunt Verna had told her, as well as the other information she had read in the history books.

Cora rocked quietly and listened, her work-worn hands

folded on her farmhouse dress. As Donna finished she shook her head slightly. "Those were hard times and long ago, Child. The good Lord knows that people have certainly found enough ways and means to kill one another. But seems to me that your great-great grandfather was ready to meet his Maker."

Donna looked at her aunt but did not say what she was thinking. Perhaps John Brown was ready to face his death, but was his daughter ready to watch it? Where was God when the little girl saw her father mercilessly killed? Or for that matter, where was He when she herself was young and wondered when her own father would come home?

Aunt Cora had a simple faith, her niece knew. She did not strictly observe the Sabbath and forbid any reading but the Bible on Sunday as did her grandmother Hogue. Nor did she make Donna memorize Scriptures as punishment as Aunt Verna had been inclined to do when she was younger. Instead, she simply trusted that God was good and wanted her to make lemonade for her niece or feed warm milk to a stray kitten.

Impulsively Donna threw her arms around her aunt. "You are good to me, Aunt Cora. I don't think you have a bad bone in your body. Or that you could even understand someone who was evil."

The older woman chuckled. "Oh, I wouldn't say I was that good, Darling. Though I can't say as I understand why someone would choose to intentionally hurt or kill another."

"You have always been kind and patient," her niece argued. "Aunt Verna has always been strict and made me sit straight and answer, "Yes, ma'am…No ma'am" and she made me sit in the corner for forever just for running down the stairs. You never did that," Donna finished, looking at her softhearted aunt with approval.

"Oh, you don't know it, but I did," her aunt said calmly.

"No! When?"

"Before you were born," she answered. "You see, in addition to me and your mother and your Uncle Nathan, there were three other boys in our family. Truth is when my first nieces and nephews came along I felt it was my duty to make sure they behaved themselves and minded their p's and q's. I'm afraid to say they thought I was a very strict old maid just the same as you think your Aunt Verna is. And likely as not Verna herself will mellow out when her younger brothers have kids."

"I would never think of you as an old maid," her niece protested.

"Why not? I am one, you know."

"Did you ever want to be married, Aunt Cora," Donna asked, remembering that Aunt Pearl had said she was once engaged.

"There was a time when I did," her aunt answered. "But that was a long time ago. I am content with what I have now."

As Donna watched the sun dipping towards the horizon she thought of Aunt Cora as a young woman, the daughter of a prosperous farmer, heading off to college in Manhattan with a beau waiting for her at home. In one season it had changed; her family's wealth diminished, her fiancé gone. Instead, she had found it was to be her destiny to keep a farmhouse and cook and clean for others.

Yet she was content. She seemed perfectly at home with the small, tidy farmhouse and the neat, clean garden. Donna wasn't sure if the farm belonged to her aunt and uncle or if they belonged to the farm. She rested her head on her aunt's shoulder, comforted by the fact that some things in life were too secure to doubt. Aunt Cora was one of them.

***

The hot days of July passed one by one. Her time at Uncle Nathan and Aunt Cora's farm was ending and she would be going to her mother's apartment in Topeka for the last week of her visit. Then she was to return to Massachusetts by train. At least, that had been the plan of others. Sometimes Donna felt her stomach twist in a knot as she anticipated the final week.

Her talk with Aunt Pearl had convinced Donna she should appeal directly to her mother. After all, what better ally could she find than her mother who had spent years trying to find her biological mother. So much depended on her visit with her mother. Yes, Mother had come out to see her when she arrived the first day and had also been out for a short time one weekend. But this would be the first time in seven years that she and her mother had been alone for more than a few hours.

As she repacked her suitcase, she wondered why she felt so tense. Of course part of her wanted to stay in Eskridge at Cora and Nathan's farm and the Hogue farm. But if her plan went the way she hoped, she would able to stay at both farms more often anyway.

Then there was Tony. She didn't want to leave him. He was getting stronger every day. Perhaps if she never had left he wouldn't have gotten sick at all. Nathan didn't think that was the case, but Donna wondered.

Of course, Topeka had many appeals of its own. Starting with warm water and electric fans, Donna thought, as she brushed her hair off her sweating face. No, as much as she loved her grandparents and aunt and uncle, she was not the farmer that Bill was. Living in Topeka with its shops and theaters, not to mention indoor plumbing, was closer to her idea of the good life. Visiting the farms and her relatives and riding Tony would make her weekends perfect once she moved back to Kansas. But best of all, she would be with her brothers again.

She thought of Marion and Kithy. Would they understand how much she loved them and needed them when she didn't come back? Would they be glad to see her on summer vacation but understand her need to be with her own mother? How could she explain to them about riding Tony and Old Bay and shelling peas with Aunt Pearl or seeing her grandmother's larkspurs grow in the shape of her name?

Donna finished packing and went outside. It was a beautiful afternoon, temperatures starting to cool after a brief summer rain. Right on schedule, Mother's car pulled up to the farmhouse in the late afternoon.

Nathan insisted on carrying Donna's luggage to Mother's car, even though she had capably handled it herself through all the train stations between Topeka and Boston. She shrugged off his old-fashioned chivalry with humor as her Mother met her on the lawn.

"My don't you look nice," she remarked to Donna. "I thought maybe the two of us could go shopping before getting a bite to eat. We could go to Pelletiers in Topeka. I thought we might look at getting you some new clothes for school."

"Sounds like fun," Donna agreed as she opened the passenger door of her mother's car. Inwardly she reflected. "It's the one thing they have in common. My stepmother takes me shopping to buy things to visit Mother. And Mother takes me shopping for clothes to wear back to live with Marion." Silently Donna crossed her fingers. Perhaps that would all change.

Donna's buoyant mood matched her mother's during the thirty-five mile trip to downtown Topeka. From her window she watched rustic farmland and small towns pass. Anticipation rose when they entered the city of Topeka and headed toward the downtown area with its crowded streets and tall buildings.

The car parked along the side of the road in front of Pelletier's Department store, housed in the seven-story Mills Building one block from the state capital. As they entered the store Donna read "1910" on the bronze plaque that announced the construction of the first steel structure in the city. Not nearly as old as some of the oldest buildings in Boston she noted. Still, shopping in Topeka was far more similar to her experience in Boston than anything the little town of Eskridge could offer.

Together they entered the double doors. Donna inhaled deeply as the aroma of leather and perfume mingled through the store. They passed hat stands and racks of purses and a glass counter filled with silk handkerchiefs on their way to the clothing department. After looking through several racks of dresses, Donna picked out a mauve colored sweater and navy blue skirt.

Happy with her new outfit, Donna walked with her mother three blocks to the Woolworth's Five and Dime. They went straight to a booth in the back of the crowded diner. The busy waitress scribbled their order for cheeseburgers on her pad. Her mother ordered a cherry coke while she asked for a large root beer float.

"Thanks for inviting me to dinner, Mother," Donna stated after the waitress headed to the kitchen. "And thanks for the clothes."

"My pleasure. I saved up some money hoping to get you an outfit while you were visiting. And I like the sweater and skirt you bought. In fact, the sweater is the same color as my wedding dress when I married your father."

This gave her the opportunity to ask a daring question. She leaned forward.

"Mother? Why did you marry Dad?"

Her mother looked at her briefly, a distant smile reflected on her face. "To be honest, I did it to get away from home."

139

"Why?"

Hazel thought for a moment. "My own mother was so strict. I wanted freedom. I wanted to do what I wanted. So I married your father thinking that would make me happy."

"Did it?" Donna asked, anticipating her mother's reaction.

"Maybe for a short time. But not long. The Depression came and we could barely put food on the table. Your father left to get work wherever he could. Sometimes he sent money home, usually he didn't. As the Depression ended and things started to get a little better, he left me and you kids for another woman."

There was silence for a few minutes as Donna sipped the frothy root beer float the waitress placed in front of her. Her thoughts whirled as her mother talked. She remembered her reaction as a child when she had heard her father was married to someone else. The initial shock had turned to dismay when she met her first stepmother and found her step-sisters were schoolmates she did not like. Donna had been ecstatic when that marriage had ended in less than a year and Aunt Cora had come to her town school to take her back to live with them on the farm.

She looked up to see her mother gazing at her. Again she saw the resemblance to the deer she had seen a few days ago. How could she describe the look? Pain? Fear? Longing?

"To be honest, I was glad when my Dad and Lenora broke up," Donna stated. "I didn't really like her. Or her daughters," she added.

"Me neither," her mother confided. "But I guess you might say I had a reason to be biased."

This was the first time her mother had spoken to her about the events that had split up their family. Their conversation was interrupted again as the white aproned waitress returned with their burgers and fries. Donna absently dipped a French fry in the ketchup.

"Marion is different than Lenora," she stated to her mother. "She and Kithy have been very good to me. I honestly think you would like them."

"Well, I'm very glad to hear they are good to you. That's all that really matters now," her mother stated. "But I have to say, my first introduction to Marion, your current stepmother, was a bit peculiar."

Donna stopped, her glass paused in midair. "What happened?" she asked.

Her mother wiped her mouth with her napkin, then grinned at her daughter. "Well, your father had divorced Lenora and was overseas fighting in the war. Then one day I got a letter from him from Europe. Imagine my surprise! I opened it and found a check. More surprise because he was not in the habit of sending money to help feed and clothe you kids. Then I unfolded the letter and found the name of three different women."

"Three women? What for?"

"He wanted me to send flowers to all three women," her mother answered. "And Easter flowers at that. Marion was one of the three women. I would have been irritated enough if he had asked me to send flowers to one woman; but three! And all that time he had never once sent money so I could buy you things you needed."

"Did you do it? Did you send them the flowers?"

Her mother laughed. "No."

"Did you send the money back to him?"

"Of course not. I bought your trombone."

"My trombone!" Donna asked in surprise. "Is that how you got it?"

"Yes is it, Darling. You wanted to play in the school marching band and there was no way I could afford a trombone. Your aunts and uncles had all done so much taking you in, buying you clothes. I don't know what would have happened to you kids without them. So I couldn't ask them for money for a band instrument. So I took his flower money and bought you the trombone," she ended with a little laugh.

Donna laughed with her. "Well, I still have my trombone. I play in the school band still. But what did Dad say when he found out?"

"He actually thanked me. He wrote back and said I had done the right thing. That was a bit of a surprise if you know your father. Anyway, Marion was one of the three women."

"Really? I wonder if Marion knew there were two others."

"I highly doubt it. And I don't think you would be doing her any particular favors to tell her now." Donna contemplated what Marion's reaction might be as she took another bite of her burger. She realized the crowd at the diner had started to thin out as the din of clattering dishes and conversations around her got quieter.

"Dad hasn't been very good to you, has he?"

"What's been, has been," Hazel said cheerfully. "No use crying over spilled milk. Or spilled husbands as the case may be."

Donna reflected on what she had heard and her mother's carefree indifference. She felt like her childhood had been a scrambled jigsaw puzzle and now the pieces were fitting into place. One piece was still missing though. How could she get herself back into the picture?

"So will you be playing your trombone in the marching band at your new high school? her mother asked as the waitress put the bill on the table. Now was the time. Donna took a deep breath.

"Well," she replied slowly, "I was considering a change of plans?"

"Oh?"

"I mean, I like being with Dad and Marion and all. But I miss you and my brothers." She saw her mother looking at her intently. "What I mean is, do you think it would be possible for me to stay in Kansas? To be close to Bill and Dick? Instead of going back to Massachusetts?"

Her mother looked at her with wide eyes. "Have you talked to your father about this?"

"Well, no."

"Who would you stay with? I don't think your Grandmother and Grandfather Hogue have room for another child with Bill and Dick in their house. And I'm not sure what your father would say about you living with Aunt Cora and Uncle Nathan again."

"I was thinking of living with you," Donna replied.

"Me?" Her mother's surprise was obvious.

"You are my mother!"

"With me? You couldn't possibly live with me!"

"Why not?"

"Why I'm getting married to Louis. We can't start our marriage with a child in the house that doesn't belong to both of us."

Donna looked at her mother incredulously. "Dad did," she stated flatly.

"That's because Marion wanted you to come live with them. Your father would allow you to live with her but not to live with me."

"Why should it make any difference if I live with my father

and stepmother or my mother and stepfather?"

"Well, it just is different," her mother replied in an annoyed tone. "First of all, it has been your father who has made all the decisions of where you kids will and won't live."

"What can he say if I want to come live with you?"

"He can say, 'No.' That's what he can say. He's done it before you know," her mother answered. "When you were younger I wanted you kids, and he refused to let you live with me. He threatened to have the courts take my kids away from me if I worked. He said I wouldn't be a fit mother if I left my kids to go to a job. But if I didn't work I couldn't feed you or pay the bills. I wanted you to live with me then. Really, I did."

"You mean you don't want me now?"

"It's not that," her mother protested. "It's your father. He would never allow it."

Donna stared at her mother, eyes wide. "Besides," Hazel continued, "I don't think Louis really wants any kids in the house."

Donna remained silent. Beneath the table she clenched her fists, barely noticing her nails digging into her skin. "I'm sorry," her mother said looking at her crestfallen face, "but there's just no way you can stay with me."

The two stared across the table at one another, neither speaking. Then Donna looked down at the table, barely noticing the crumbs she brushed from her lap.

"You'll have to go back to your father in Massachusetts," her mother finished. "There's just no other way."

Sending Me Back

A long, pent-up sigh escaped from Donna as she looked blankly out the window of the train, not seeing the country passing before her. A novel lay unopened on her lap, a parting gift from Aunt Cora. She had no interest in reading.

She stared unseeing out the train window, absent-mindedly wrapping her hair around her finger, recounting the last days of her trip.

She had stayed with Mother in Topeka as planned, attending her mother's nightly social events. They hadn't talked any more about her remaining in Kansas. Oh they had talked about other things and Donna had smiled and laughed as her mother did, chatting with Hazel's friends. She met Louis who declared Donna to be "pretty and charming."

"Pretty and charming," Donna thought with disgust. "What's so charming about mindless chatter when your heart is breaking and no one cares?" Certainly he didn't.

"So that's it," Donna thought as she sat on the train. "My mother has her new boyfriend or fiancé - whatever he is. And she doesn't want me interfering. So she's sending me back."

"Sending me back. Sending me back." The clatter of the train mimicked the voice in her head.

Donna nervously twirled her hair around her finger. She had journeyed to Topeka with a purpose. Or perhaps there were two purposes. She wanted to know why she had been separated from her mother years before. And she wanted to live with her again.

Piece by piece her relatives had helped her put the puzzle of her childhood back together. But the hole in the middle of the puzzle felt like a hole in her heart. She would not be staying in Kansas where she belonged. Her mother didn't want her. Her father wouldn't let her go. She was powerless.

With a sudden awareness, Donna realized how the doe and her mother were alike. They were both powerless.

"Mother's new fiancé doesn't want me living with them now. My father wouldn't let me live with her before," she reflected. It was, after all, to her father – and not her mother – that Bill had insisted he would not move to Massachusetts. Did her mother not care enough about her children to put her foot down the way Bill had done? Or was she simply too powerless?

And why did her father dictate where she would live, even when he had been out of the country in the war and others had taken care of her? She remembered her uncle's words. "To show everyone that he can," he said. Of course, he was talking about the antelope racing the train, not her father. Like the antelope her father was daring and reckless, quick to show others he was the one in charge.

Donna sighed again, resting her head against the window, resigned to the fact she was returning. It wouldn't be bad to go back to East Bridgewater and the high school there, she reasoned. She had her friends, particularly her best friend Janie. And Marion and Kithy wanted her. Perhaps there was consolation in that, since her own mother didn't seem to care. At least not much.

She would miss both the farms of course. And Tony. His health had improved but she could not be certain her pony would still be alive when she next returned to Kansas, whenever that might be. Aunt Cora and Grandma and Grandpa Hogue would always be there for her no matter how long she might be away. Of course, nobody lived forever, she knew, but life without them was unimaginable.

But her brothers? Donna bit her lip. It had been so long since she had seen Dick she had barely known him. Who would he be when they met again? Her younger brother was so small and vulnerable in contrast to her older brother Bill. He was strong and quiet, like their father in many ways, but much more dependable. No matter how long they were separated she would always know Bill.

But her dreams of seeing him on the weekends, watching him play football, and hanging out with his crowd were gone. What's worse, she had been in Kansas most of the time he had been visiting Massachusetts and working with their father.

"At least I'll see him for a few weeks before he returns to the Midwest," she decided, somewhat comforted by the thought. But even that little comfort would be denied when she discovered what changes awaited her and her brothers.

Return to Massachusetts

"It's good to have you back." Kithy was saying. In honor of Donna's return to Massachusetts, they were eating at the Joppa Grill. She was seated next to Bill. Her father and Marion sat on the other side of the white linen-covered table. Even at a restaurant, Kithy sat at the head of the table.

Donna turned to her brother, "Have you ever been to Joppa before?" He shook his head in reply. "It's one of my favorite restaurants," his sister informed him. "Dad and Marion took me here the first night I moved to Massachusetts."

"Been pretty busy working evenings," he explained.

"I love their breadsticks," she said reaching for another breadstick from the basket, "and their fruit cups. People come from miles to get their breadsticks."

Bill nodded his approval as he took another breadstick himself.

"Have you been to Plymouth yet?" his sister inquired.

"Nope," he answered.

"Well we ought to go while you are here. Kithy and I like to go to Bert's Cove to eat when we are in Plymouth. Don't we Kithy?"

"Yes we do," Kithy said with a grin. "Though the truth is, I like to eat just about everywhere."

"They do have good food," Marion added, "but Mom also

148

likes to get a seat there and watch the ocean waves. Did you know my great grandfather, Robert Keith, owned the land Bert's Cove is on?"

"Really?" Donna asked.

"That's ocean front property!" her father remarked. "He must have sold it for a pretty penny."

"One hundred dollars," Marion answered.

"For land right on the Atlantic Beach!" her father remarked. "He sold it cheap."

"Keep in mind," Kithy chuckled, "that one hundred dollars used to be worth, well, one hundred dollars. It was a lot of money back then."

"I'll admit I was taken back when I saw the deed after my father's death," Marion countered. "All the property along the beach is valuable. With the tourists coming to Plymouth they have something going there."

"Sounds like it," Bill added.

"Yes, we will have to make a trip to Plymouth before Bill returns to Kansas," Kithy stated. She turned to her son-in-law. "Howard, you are going to have to give the boy some time off long enough to do a little road trip with us to Plymouth." Donna looked at her step-grandmother at the head of the table who winked at her. She smiled back.

"By the way you are eating," continued Kithy, "I'd say the fresh Kansas air must have done you some good."

"Fresh air and good farm cooking," her father interjected. "I'd be willing to bet my mother made some good meals while you were there."

"She did. Aunt Cora did too."

The three adults listened as Donna told about her visit. Howard wanted to hear about his parents' farm. Kithy asked about the daily routines and food on the menu. Marion was curious about her relatives and what Donna had done with them.

Only one subject about her trip was off limits: her mother. "What would they think if they knew I asked to live with her instead of returning?" she wondered. "I will never tell them I asked," she pledge silently.

She laughed at Bill's expression when the waitress served her father a well-done crisp steak, and her step-mother a lightly browned rare one.

"Opposites attract," Kithy quipped.

"I would have missed them all if I hadn't come back," she realized. Still she felt a nagging discomfort.

Why was it Kithy always sat at the head of the table? Why did her father listen to her and no one else? Marion and her father continued eating their meal comfortably. Bill was his usual quiet self. Donna was aware of Kithy watching her closely.

***

"So tell me," Kithy quizzed her a few days later, "did your grandmother and aunt have you dust when you were in Kansas?" Kithy was sitting in her favorite easy chair at one end of the long formal living room watching as Donna completed her chore.

"Aunt Cora? Well, yes, of course I helped with dusting at her house since I stayed with her," Donna replied. "I also helped in the barn with the farm chores. But at Grandma Hogue's house I only did the dishes."

Kithy inquired about the tasks she had done around the farm. As Donna carefully dusted the figurines on the fireplace mantel, she described the barn and the milk separators. She talked about Tony and her concerns for him. Kithy listened with interest.

"I imagine it was difficult for you to leave your pony," Kithy commented, "particularly before you were certain he was to recover. Though I'm sure," she added, "that your grandfather's medicine was probably just what he needed."

Donna found comfort in Kithy's empathy. "It was hard," she answered, "hard to leave Tony, and Aunt Cora, and Grandma and Grandpa Hogue, and my, well, everybody."

Kithy leaned back in her chair watching her. Perhaps she had noticed Donna had almost mentioned her mother.

"I'm sure it is hard," Kithy reflected. "Hard to leave the people you belong to."

"And hard to have your fate decided by others," Donna answered. "You can't imagine what that's like."

"Oh? You think that would be unknown to me?" Kithy asked leaning forward again.

Donna looked around the room. The floral carpeting, the oil painting of one of Marion's ancestors, the grandfather clock; all reflected a life of ease. While they were not wealthy, Kithy and Marion were proud of the fact that they were descended from the first families in Massachusetts and had ancestors that had sailed on the Mayflower. What would they know of the kind of hardships her farming family had to undergo? The disease of livestock that destroyed a family's wealth, the failed crops of the Depression, the chores that started hours before a child's long hike to school?

"What are you holding in your hand, Donna?" her step-grandmother asked her.

Held in the palm of her hand was a porcelain figure of a crawling baby. Curly haired, blue eyes, rosy cheeks, wearing an old fashioned white gown; Donna had never paid more attention to it than dusting required.

"It's a baby," Donna answered. "It looks old."

"Yes," her grandmother chuckled, "old it is. Rather pretty, too. But all that glitters is not gold. You see, you don't have to live on a Midwest farm to know hard times. We may have some pretty knick-knacks and a cozy home. But the truth is my mother was an indentured servant."

"Yep," the older woman continued seeing the question in Donna's face. "Some might even say she was a slave."

Part 5

The Free & The Brave

The Land of the Free and the Brave

All hail to Massachusetts,
The land of the free and the brave!
For Bunker Hill and Charlestown,
And flag we love to wave:
For Lexington and Concord,
And the shot heard 'round the world;
All hail to Massachusetts,
We'll keep her flag unfurled.
She stands upright for freedom's light
That shines from sea to sea:
All hail to Massachusetts!
Our country 'tis of thee!

Massachusetts State Song

Hard to Be Brave

1861
Boston

Overhead seagulls circled and dove into the water. The sounds of their cries mixed with the sound of waves and the noises from the wharf. Horns of ships, shouts of people, and the clang of metal accented the air.

A young girl about nine years old was standing with her mother. The girl was watching the birds. She inhaled the smell of salt water and enjoyed the mist as it splashed her every time a wave came to shore. She looked up at her mother who was focused on the ships in the harbor.

Her mother gasped. "Look, Mary, there he is," she said pointing. "Your father is on that ship."

Mary looked to the structure her mother pointed. The frame of a tall ship was on the outskirts of the wharf. Her mother liked to come down to the shore-line and see the ships, but a recent illness had kept them away for several weeks.

"Is it going to be a big ship?" the little girl asked eyeing the frame of the ship.

"Yes. But they all seem like big ships to me."

Mary dug her shoes into the sand and watched a crab nearby. Then her attention went back to the water. "Tell me the story of the important ship," Mary demanded.

It was her favorite story and she heard it many times. One hundred and three people on a small ship came from England

and were the first white people in Massachusetts. They came on the Mayflower, and wrote their own laws called the Mayflower Compact, and made friends with the Indians who helped them. And no matter how many times she heard it; there was always something else to learn.

"The Pilgrims actually started out in two ships," her mother explained this time. "They were named the Mayflower and the Speedwell. But the Speedwell was not seaworthy, and so it had to turn back. That's why your father's job as a shipbuilder is so important. People's lives are dependent on a ship being safe through all the storms When they found out the Speedwell wasn't safe, all the people on-board needed to leave it and get on the Mayflower making it even more crowded. Can you imagine, Mary? All those people on board a ship half the size of those there in the harbor? "

No, Mary couldn't imagine it. She had never been to sea herself though she had been on ships several times. Her father had taken her on-board ships anchored in the harbor as they were nearly completed. If she could sail and choose the rooms, she would choose the captain's quarters. But the Pilgrims didn't get to go in the captain's quarters.

Mary watched the waves wash to shore and then spread back toward the sea. It was easy to see why that ship had come to Massachusetts. The water would bring it here. Ever since Mary could remember the waves had rushed toward her on the beach. All the waves in the world headed toward Boston, so it was only natural the Mayflower would have come here, Mary reasoned.

As a long "gong" sounded from the wharf, Mary noticed a change in the sounds and movement. Men were leaving their posts and moving to go home. That meant her father would walk up to them soon. Her mother started to wave her lace handkerchief. Mary turned in the direction she was facing and saw her father approaching.

"There's my girls," he said as Mary reached his side. He picked her up and hugged her. She brushed saw dust from his hair. In turn, he tousled her long curls as he always did.

"I love how your mother fixes your curls," he had said once. "I'm going to get a portrait painted of my two girls." That was a few months ago before mother had become ill. Now that she was better, maybe they would get the portrait done as he had promised.

"It's good to see you are strong enough to come down," he stated to his wife. Together they walked to Cornhill, the neighborhood in Boston where they lived. Mary raced ahead, happy to walk through the town with both her parents again.

The next day was rainy and overcast. Mary sat looking out the window. She hated being stuck inside. She sighed and picked up the sampler on her lap.

No matter how hard she tried, she could not make the pretty, even stitches her mother made. Though she kept trying, the threads split and turned to knots. She looked at her sampler. It did not look right.

"Practice makes perfect," her mother had told her. "It took a long time for me to make beautiful stitches." It was hard to imagine that her mother's beautiful lace and perfect stitches ever looked as bad as this.

Noise out on the road caught her attention. The street was only a few feet from the front of the houses in their neighborhood. Mary glanced out the window and saw a group of men carrying someone. They were coming toward their door.

"Mother," she called. But her mother had already rushed to the door and opened it.

Five or six men came in carrying someone. Mary gasped.

It was her father. They carried him in and laid him on the table.

"Father," Mary cried, rushing to his side. He did not answer her. His hair was matted with blood. His eyes were closed and his breathing uneven.

"Bad accident. Fell from the mast," one of the men was telling her mother.

The rest of the day was a blur for Mary. Neighbors came and moved her father from the table to his bed. She never left his side. A doctor was called and came to the house.

"It was a bad fall," the doctor said. "We'll see how he does through the night."

Night came. Mary must have fallen asleep and someone carried her to bed. She woke the next morning wondering why she was still in her clothes.

Then she remembered her father. "We'll see how he does through the night," the doctor had said. She rushed out of her room into the living room. There her mother sat staring.

Their neighbor walked up to Mary. "Can you be brave, little Miss Mary?" she asked.

No, Mary could not be brave. How could she be, when the world was so big and she was so little?

"Your father died a few hours ago," the neighbor continued. "You are going to have to be strong and help your mother now."

Mary must have said something. She didn't know what. She went to her mother and laid her head on her lap. She felt her mother's fingers in her long curls. They cried together.

***

The sun wanted to shine. It had rained the last several days and the afternoon breeze had a chill. Still, Mary wanted to sit outside her house for a little longer.

Her mood was somber. She sat on the porch, barely noticing the coming and going in their busy city neighborhood.

Since her father's death everything had changed. They never went to the wharf anymore. Her mother stopped eating. Neighbors told her she must eat to get stronger. She didn't want to eat. Mary missed her mother's smile. Her once shining eyes were dull.

And now she was too sick to get up. Her neighbor came over to help. There wasn't much else to do inside. Or outside either. She had brought out some paper and a pencil to draw. Across the street she could see some flowers in a window box.

That gave Mary an idea. Maybe a picture of flowers would make her mother feel better. With more ambition, her pencil moved faster on the page.

"Miss Mary, your lunch is ready," the voice of her neighbor caused her to look up. Miss Mary. That was what her father had always called her.

"I'm here," the little girl answered.

"Come in, Child. Your food will get cold," the neighbor admonished. "What's that you have drawn? Flowers? Very pretty."

"They are for my mother."

"That's very thoughtful of you, Miss Mary. But your mother is quite sick today."

"Can I bring her my picture?" Mary asked.

Before an answer was given, a knock on the door was heard. The neighbor hurried to open it, and then stepped outside.

Mary heard voices from the other side of the door. Quietly she ate her soup. It was the neighbor's voice and a man's voice. What were they talking about?

The door opened and a man came in with her neighbor. Mary recognized him as the doctor that had come when her father had fallen. He nodded to her and went into her mother's room. The neighbor followed leaving Mary alone in the kitchen.

"Is my mother that sick?" Mary wondered, remembering the doctor had come before her father died. Fear gripped her inside as the spoon slid from her hand. She stared at her soup without seeing it. "Does the doctor only come when people die?" she asked herself.

No, she remembered the doctor's visit to their home last year when she was sick. Chicken pox the doctor had called it. He came last winter when Irvin next door broke his leg. Maybe mother would be all right.

Leaving the lunch things on the table, she moved quietly to the chair by the window. A gentle rain was falling. A door opened and footsteps came toward her. Without turning, she heard the doctor's voice talking to her neighbor. "This is hard," she heard him say.

Mary heard the neighbor whisper something low, and the doctor left the house. The neighbor came and sat by Mary.

"Is my mother very sick?" Mary asked.

"My dear child," the woman answered slowly. "I am so sorry to tell you this, but your mother is dead."

Mary said nothing.

"We tried. But we could not break her fever. "

Mary stared at the window, without seeing. This time, there was no one to hug and cry with her. There was no mother to run her fingers through her hair.

"My hair," thought Mary. "Who will make my curls now?" There would be no portrait of her and her mother as her father once had promised.

Others came. Someone cleared the lunch things and washed them. Mary did not know who. An important looking man came and looked at her. Mary had seen him before. He was often on the wharf, and always looked so busy and in charge.

"There are no relations to take her," the neighbor was telling the man.

She heard him say there were too many debts. She had heard her mother talk about debts after her father died. Mary didn't know what debts were. She had wondered why there were too many of them since she had never seen them. She still didn't know.

"The house will have to be sold," the man was saying. "That will take care of the debts, but not much else."

"And the child?" someone asked.

"She will have to be auctioned off," the man was telling the neighbor. She heard her neighbor gasp.

Auctioned off? Mary once heard her parents talking about two brothers found on the wharf who had been auctioned off. To prevent the orphan boys from starving or getting into trouble, her father had explained, the city held an auction and the boys went to the homes of the two lowest bidders. The city paid the families that took the boys the amount they bid for their food and upkeep every year until they were adults. A farmer had bid low for the older, stronger brother since he could work and earn his keep. In fact several families had bid on the older brother. But the younger boy was weak; not as many were interested in him. The city had to pay more for a family to take him. Mary remembered her mother fretting that the two brothers were going to be separated. She had often wondered if the two boys ever got to see each other.

"Now I'm the one who is going to be auctioned." Mary thought. She ran her fingers through her hair. The curls were not as soft as they were when her mother used to fix them. Maybe no one would bid for her since she didn't have pretty hair. Oh how she longed for her father's strong arms and her mother's gentle touch.

"She can stay with me until the auction," the neighbor was saying.

"They are going to sell me," Mary said to herself. She had never felt so alone.

No Home of My Own

1884

"We're almost there Mrs. Howard. Only a couple more blocks."

Two women sat in an open carriage pulled by a pair of grey, dappled horses. The younger woman, plainly dressed, was driving the team. Next to her sat an older woman whose white hair was pulled in a tight bun and covered with a wide brimmed hat. She had a fur coat and matching fur trimmed gloves. In spite of her stylish attire, it appeared from the look on her face that she was not enjoying herself.

"I can see for myself it is only a couple of blocks," the older woman snapped. "I've been making this drive to town for decades."

"Yes ma'am, I know you have," the younger woman responded soothingly. "But these horses seem quite anxious to get us into town this morning."

Mrs. Howard merely mumbled an answer. The carriage slowed down as the younger woman guided the team to a building near the middle of the block of businesses that lined the street. She got down from the carriage herself. As she was tying the horses, she noticed from the corner of her eye a lone form approaching the side of the carriage.

"Good morning, Mrs. Howard," stated a young man offering his hand to the fur-trimmed woman still in the carriage. "May I help you down?"

163

"Well I thank you, Mr. Atwell," answered the older woman, taking the man's arm and dismounting from her carriage. "You are not working in the blacksmith shop today?"

The younger woman looked on and stifled the smile that might betray her amusement watching her employer adjust her gloves and hat while she addressed the coatless man in front of her. He had the sleeves of his white muslin shirt rolled up, covered by a leather vest unique to his trade, apparently indifferent to the crisp morning air.

"Just finished delivering a large order of railings to the Robertsons," he answered the query. "I worked late through the night making them so I'm heading home now."

"You must be tired if you have been up all night then. Mary Ann and I have an appointment at the hair salon this morning. Are you ready, Mary Ann?"

"Might as well cancel your appointments," shrugged the blacksmith. "You both look fine to me." He glanced at the long, chestnut curls and pink complexion of the younger woman, his walrus mustache turned up in a smile, eyes sparkling with good-natured humor.

"Flattery will get you nowhere, Mr. Atwell," argued Mrs. Howard, noting the rising color in her younger companion's cheeks. "Come, Mary Ann, we will be late."

The woman called Mary Ann nodded to the man and took the arm of Mrs. Howard. As they walked toward the nearby salon out of his hearing, Mary Ann spoke for the first time.

"It is just you that has an appointment with the hair dresser, Mrs. Howard. Once you are comfortable there, I was thinking of doing some shopping myself."

"Oh, are you?" the woman asked. "Or did you have hopes of meeting someone? Mr. Atwell, for instance?"

"Oh, no ma'am," Mary Ann answered quickly, her cheeks

blushing. "I had not made any arrangements to see Mr. Atwell or anyone else this morning. I was hoping," she continued, "to get a small gift for Garaphilia for her birthday."

"I guess you needn't stay beside me while I get my hair done then," the woman answered. "I wouldn't want to ruin your plans. Though really, your salary is intended to cover your personal expenses and I daresay Garaphilia would not be expecting you to spend money on her."

"Oh I feel so bad for Garaphilia, after losing the baby. I know how devastated she was. I was thinking something colorful might brighten her birthday, if only just a little bit."

"So be it," sighed Mrs. Howard as they entered the door. "I expect I will be here at least about an hour. You can meet me back here then."

"Oh I don't think it will take me that long," responded Mary Ann cheerfully. "I'll be back before you are done." She held the door open, and seeing the hair stylist come forward to greet Mrs. Howard, withdrew back toward the street.

"I'll try the corner store," she thought to herself. "I saw a music box in there that would be just perfect." She headed down the road.

"Going somewhere special?" a familiar voice interrupted her thoughts. She turned to see the young blacksmith watching her.

"Now, why did you have to go and make her suspicious?" she asked him.

"Ashamed to be seen with me?" he asked, his mustache twitching in amusement. He fell into pace beside her.

"No, I am not 'ashamed' to be seen with anybody," she retorted. "I just prefer not to be interrogated by Mrs. Howard." Mary Ann held her chin high and hoped it would convey displeasure. "I would appreciate it," she said giving a sharp tone to her voice, "if you did not go around rousing the suspicions of my employer."

"It just so happens that I've shod many an angry and stubborn mule. Too many to fear the pretended wrath of a young damsel. Or," he added with a smirk, "the genuine wrath of her old dowager."

"Horace!" she exclaimed in shock, looking over her shoulder to assure herself no one would had heard. She turned to look him squarely in the eyes. He faced her without a trace of uncertainty.

His confidence unnerved her. She had turned away many a suitor in the last few years with barely a word of dismissal. But Horace's strong frame and firm gaze indicated no intent of being turned away.

"I was serious last week when I asked you to marry me," he stated quietly.

Mary Ann shook her head as a slow sigh escaped her. "Can't you understand? I just can't leave Mrs. Howard now."

"She needs you? You and only you?"

"You just saw her. She wouldn't be able to get to town on her own. She's getting older you see," Mary Ann explained.

He guffawed. "Yes, I see she's getting older. The population tends to do that, you know. It's not exactly a reason for the younger generation not to get married. In fact, it seems…."

"Please do stop it," Mary Ann pleaded in exasperation. "She needs my help. She is used to being independent and having her own home. And she is terribly afraid of me leaving her."

"She has her own daughters," he observed.

"Amanda and Garaphilia are married and have families of their own. And Sarah died a few years ago. That was devastating for all of us."

"Undoubtedly. And her son? Last I knew he did not have a

wife. Can he not help look after his own dear mother?"

Mary Ann laughed quietly. "While Henry may have been the pride of his mother's heart, he has not actually lived up to their expectations. He is always been very weak and…"

"Lazy?" Horace finished the sentence for her.

"That too." Mary Anne agreed. "I'm afraid Mrs. Howard's life would be rather dull and cramped if she had to depend on her son for any assistance of any kind."

"But her own daughters," observed the man, "they were able to marry – and I daresay she not only let them marry she actively searched for appropriate suitors. So why is marriage to be denied you?"

"Why can't you understand?" she asked him. "She needs me. And honestly, if it weren't for her and Mr. Howard I can't bear to think what would have happened to me."

The two had wandered to a low wall and he perched on it.

"Mary Ann, it saddens me to think of you as an orphan alone in the world. I'm glad the Howards brought you here to our little village of West Bridgewater and you weren't left begging on the streets of Boston. But why do you feel so loyal to them now? Mrs. Howard doesn't exactly strike me as the loving, motherly type?"

"Well, I have to agree she isn't a motherly figure. She certainly didn't replace my own mother whom I missed so very, very much," Mary Ann said slowly.

After a brief pause, he interrupted her thoughts. "In the blacksmith shop we see everyone – rich, poor, everyone in between. I've always had mixed feelings about the Overseers of the Poor and the way they auction children off to the lowest bidder. It's better than leaving people to starve of course. But on the other hand, shipping children off to be serving girls to the likes of Mrs. Howard seems a bit – well, cruel."

"No, no, I can't say she was cruel to me," Mary Ann objected. "Strict yes. I remember the day I came. She showed me to my room and explained my chores. The jobs they gave me at first weren't that hard really, and I tried to please them. But Mrs. Howard was so difficult to please. Her dark eyes would narrow and I would get quite a tongue lashing if I didn't do things to suit her. But she never hit me."

"How heroic of her," Horace commented dryly. "And that has earned her a lifelong commitment of servitude?"

"It was Mr. Howard," Mary Ann continued, ignoring his interruption. "He always had a kind word for me and called me his Little Mary. My own father called me Miss Mary so it made me feel at home somehow. Oh how much I needed his kindness." She looked away, hoping he wouldn't notice the quiver in her voice.

Another quiet interlude followed. Horace reflected, "You have been with their family for over 20 years now."

"Yes, they kept me on. I don't really have an education to get a job, you know. And I do know how to keep house to suit Mrs. Howard now. That was knowledge dearly bought I must say. Their daughters have always been so kind to me. And I promised Mr. Howard in his last illness that I would take care of Mrs. Howard."

She turned to face him. "How could I do any less? Would you have me break a promise I made to the man who took care of me and was kind to me when I was all alone?"

"No," said Horace slowly. He took her hands in his. "My dear, Mary Ann, I have a hard time believing that kind Mr. Howard intended you to never marry, never have a home or family of your own, to live as a serving girl all of your life. Is that what he wanted and asked you to promise?"

"I promised to look after Mrs. Howard. A promise is a

promise, Horace. While Mrs. Howard is alive, I must help her."

For the first time, an angry look flashed across his eyes, then disappeared. He cleared his throat and stood up.

"Very well. It's not what I wanted you to say, of course. I will be moving to Nantucket, and I was hoping you would come as my wife."

"Nantucket!"

"Yes, I have been offered a job there."

"Nantucket?"

"Yes, I said Nantucket. That's an island not far from Boston. You could be returning to your childhood home. But this time with me."

"I want to Horace. Really I do. But Mrs. Howard, I just can't leave her. In fact, I need to get back to her soon. She will fret if I'm not there when she is ready to go home."

She saw his mustache twitch again. This time, it was from anger, not humor.

"Well, I hope you and Mrs. Howard are very happy together" he said curtly.

"Oh, please don't be angry!"

"Angry? I guess I have no reason to be angry. You have made your decision and I have made mine." He turned and sauntered off.

***

The trip back home was quiet. Mary Ann had little to say, and Mrs. Howard was content with her own thoughts. She glanced at her out of the corner of her eye. "She has no idea what I'm giving up for her," Mary Ann thought.

But maybe she did. For the last several months Mrs. Howard jealously guarded the young woman's time. Even as a teenager, Mary Ann was free to socialize with her friends – as long as she got her work done first.

But lately she had to give an account of where she was going and who she had been with when she left the house. Just two weeks ago Mrs. Howard had bemoaned her fear that, "You will up and desert me." Mary Ann had pledged her loyalty to stay as long as she was needed.

"I'll always be needed," Mary Ann thought now. Horace's statements nagged at her. Was there anything wrong with her having a home and family of her own? Mrs. Howard seemed to think so.

Back at their home, Mary Ann began dinner. She would bake a cake for Garaphilia's birthday. But her pleasure at having Mrs. Howard's two daughters come home had been dampened.

"He's moving to Nantucket," she whispered under her breath. "When will I see him again?"

***

The fall months passed and the chill in the air hinted that winter would not be long in coming. Mary Ann was sorting and cleaning the cranberries that had been picked the day before. Vats of boiling water were waiting on the stove for the bitter berries. Mary Ann had always loved making cranberry juice and cranberry jelly. Even as a child she was entertained by the popping sound the berries made as they were boiled.

But today a long sigh escaped her lips. The fruit had no appeal as she noted her fingers stained red. She would have to wash the red dye off. "But," she surmised, "who really cares what color my fingers are anyway." Since Horace Atwell had left for Nantucket, Mary Ann had less interest in her appearance.

The sound of the horses returning caught her attention.

Mrs. Howard and her son had ridden to town together. She straightened her apron automatically as her mistress entered the kitchen.

"Well, I do say, Mary Ann. I have had a bit of news to-day. Are you putting those cranberries in before the water is thoroughly boiling? Henry and I were just to town and we saw Mrs. Atwell, Horace's mother. He moved to Nantucket only a few months ago as I'm sure you know. I hope you did get all of the twigs and leaves out of those cranberries. Anyway, as I was saying, Mrs. Atwell just got a letter from her son."

"Mother!" called Henry. "Where do you want me to carry your packages?"

Mary Ann tried to move slowly and deliberately. She could feel the color rising in her cheeks so she turned toward the hot water. It wouldn't do to hurry Mrs. Howard or interrupt. She stirred the pot in a wide careful arch, hoping no one would notice her tension.

"You may put them in my room please, Henry," his mother answered. "Now, where was I?"

"Mrs. Atwell received a letter," Mary Ann reminded her calmly.

"Oh yes, the letter. Well, it seems like Mr. Atwell has got himself engaged. Must be having quite a time in Nantucket, I wouldn't wonder."

Mary Ann dropped the spoon. She stifled the cry she felt.

"Do be careful, Mary Ann," Mrs. Howard remarked. "We don't need any medical bills. Your eye glasses cost us enough you know. But ever since you got sick with diphtheria when you were eleven we have had to get them. Mr. Howard insisted on it. Of course, I would have it no other way."

"Yes, ma'am," Mary Ann mumbled.

"Anyway, as I was saying, Mrs. Atwell is all worked up with

news that Horace will be getting married and having his fiancé come home for the holidays. But that's not the way we do it in this family, I can tell you that."

Henry entered the kitchen. "I carried your smaller packages to your room as you asked," he announced.

"And the crate?" his mother queried.

"That's heavy," the son protested. "That's why you pay servants," he stated, nodding toward Mary Ann. He started to turn away then spun around to look at her again.

"What's wrong with you, anyway?" he asked Mary Ann bluntly.

"I've been standing over these vats all morning," Mary Ann responded quickly. "Watch them for a minute, I'll get your things in the house."

Without waiting for a reply, she crossed the kitchen and left the house. "Honestly, Henry," she could hear the mother saying. She heard nothing else.

Outside of the house Mary Ann approached the carriage. Without any curiosity, she lifted the crate and carried it toward the house. In times past she had been both disgusted and offended at the son's inability to work, but now it escaped her attention all together. She was glad for a chance to get away from them both.

After leaving the crate in Mrs. Howard's room, Mary Ann walked down the hall into her own plain bedroom. She got a glimpse of herself in the mirror. Her hair was askew, glasses fogged, apron stained from the days chores.

She yanked the apron off and let it fall to the floor. She sat on the bed and covered her face with her hands. She didn't cry. She wouldn't cry.

"Mary Ann," she could hear Mrs. Howard call. "The cranberries will get overcooked."

She squared her shoulders. "Apparently," she said to herself, "it was not intended that I should ever have a home of my own."

***

A gentle snow was falling, blanketing the farm house in a quiet hush. Inside the fire crackled. Mary Ann looked at the tall Christmas tree. For some reason she couldn't explain, the Christmas tree always reminded her of the parents she lost when she was young.

"No pine cones?" Henry asked.

"No," she answered quietly. "No pine cones."

Her own mother had decorated their home with pine cones and berries and pine wreathes in the days before Christmas. On her first Christmas with the Howards she had brought in a handful of pine cones and put them on the tree. It seemed like the thing to do; the thing her mother would have done.

But apparently the Howards didn't put pine cones on the tree. Henry had fussed, and Mrs. Howard had started to remove them. Then she had looked at Mary Ann. Her hand was touching a pine cone, but froze in midair as she looked at Mary Ann's face. The matron gave Mary Ann the "deep" look as Mary Ann called it. Her eyebrows arched, almost touching her hairline.

The pine cones remained on the tree – that year and every year after. No one knew why Mary Ann put them there, she didn't even know herself. They certainly weren't as colorful as the glass ornaments that Mrs. Howard so carefully had purchased.

But this year there were no pine cones. Mary Ann simply wasn't interested in gathering them and decorating. She looked at the tree. It stirred up memories almost too painful too remember.

There was that first Christmas without her parents. She had been brought to this warm, cheerful house. In this home of a successful butcher, she had never hungered for food. And the holidays brought the Howard sisters back to their parents' home. Mary Ann had longed for the gatherings that brought Amanda, and Sarah, and Garaphilia back to the house. The friends and beaus brought bustle and laughter to the usually quiet home. Even though she waited on the guests and didn't get to take part in the activities, having the girls come home was the highlight of her life.

And they brought trinkets for her – outgrown clothes, old jewelry, knick knacks from their travels. They enjoyed brightening the life of the orphan child who had come into their family.

Toys she did not have. The presents the Howards gave her on Christmas and her birthday were simple: clothes, shoes, and life's basic necessities. She was not indulged, but neither was she neglected. Many orphans had fared much worse.

Then there was the Christmas when she had the diphtheria. Mrs. Howard had called the doctor. She also had called for Sarah to come home. Sarah came. She read stories and talked to Mary Ann. And, of course, there was kind Mr. Howard who insisted she do no work until she was completely well.

It was Mrs. Howard who discovered that Mary Ann could not see well after she recovered. She had always been quick to scold if the housework was not done properly, but after several scoldings she gave the child that deep look. She whispered something to Mr. Howard, who had taken Mary Ann outside to ask what she could see on the other side of the large, well-cared for garden. He discovered she needed glasses.

Mrs. Howard was the one who saw Mary Ann looking at

embroidery. Stitching was one chore that Mary Ann had not been expected to do in her new home. Braiding straw, knitting scarves, darning socks, in addition to the constant cleaning and cooking, were the skills Mary Ann acquired. But such fine work as embroidery or painting were not on the list of things she was called to do.

But on one Saturday shopping trip, Mary Ann ran her fingers over the sampler at the general store, unaware that Mrs. Howard was scrutinizing her actions. The orphan girl was wondering the destiny of the intricate samplers embroidered by her own mother. Her face flushed when she looked up and saw Mrs. Howard's penetrating eyes watching her. Soon after, needle, thread, and a pattern were waiting for her. Mrs. Howard critically examined the stitching the child had done with her dark snapping eyes, but she held her tongue and didn't scold. With painstaking practice, Mary Ann's embroidery slowly started looking like something her own mother might have made.

Unfortunately, the matron's fierce temper had blazed and her sharp tongue unleashed when she found simple drawings left by the young girl. Mary Ann had seen sketches and been amazed that trees and houses and people could come to life on a piece of paper with nothing but a pencil. Mrs. Howard was indignant that Mr. Howard's stationery should be wasted on such frivolous sketches, though Mr. Howard himself was unperturbed by such a trivial infraction. But then Mrs. Howard had looked more carefully at Mary Ann's sketch of a tree and arched her eyebrows. Thereafter, there was always plenty of plain paper in the kitchen and no objection was made when she would take a pencil and paper and go outside to draw.

The years had ticked by. The girls moved further away. Mary Ann had become a teenager and a very proficient housekeeper – even by the exacting standards of Mrs. Howard. But she had longed for friends her own age.

Once she was invited to a party. There was dancing and she loved it: the music, the swaying, the carefree friends. But, oh what if Mrs. Howard were to find out that she, Mary Ann, had been to a dance. Mrs. Howard belonged to the New Jerusalem church and dancing was not accepted.

Mrs. Howard did find out.

To Mary Ann's surprise she simply looked at her with eyebrows arched. "If you want to go dancing with your friends at night," she had said, "I'll expect you to get up early to get your work done."

Thereafter Mary Ann got up at 5:00 in the morning so her chores would be done inside and in the garden. And true to her word, Mrs. Howard never scolded if Mary Ann joined her friends to go dancing.

When Mary Ann turned twenty one she was free to go where she would. But without schooling, she had no place to go. What could she do but keep house? Mr. and Mrs. Howard wanted her to stay with them, and a small salary of two dollars a week was given to her.

Several times would-be suitors had come to the house, seeking any sign of encouragement from Mary Ann, which she did not give them. Mrs. Howard's eyes scrutinized every feature of such gentlemen, but she had made no complaint. Mr. Howard had thought it inevitable that the artistic young woman with curly chestnut hair and kind though weak eyes would attract attention among the town's people her own age.

But now Mr. Howard was gone, and Mrs. Howard depended on her more and more to help her with the house. Sarah had died, and the visits from Garaphilia and Amanda were less frequent.

But Christmas they all came back. It was a special time.

176

She was no longer an orphan girl, but part of the family. Yet something inside of her had been empty. She dreamed of a home of her own, like she had when her mother and father had lived in Boston. And living not so far from Boston now was Horace. If only they could be together.

No. She mustn't think about it. She pulled herself from the tree and went into the kitchen. "Garaphilia will be arriving soon. I'll get some cider heated," she called over her shoulder.

Pouring the cider into a pan, she heard the crunch of footsteps outside. "Are they here already?" she asked herself. A figure was coming toward the back door, and Mary Ann hurried to open it.

She found herself face to face with Horace Atwell.

"Horace?"

He stomped his boots on the porch and pushed his way into the warm kitchen. Snow glistened on his hair and shoulders.

"Mary Ann. I couldn't wait to come back and see you." He took both his hands in hers.

"But, I heard, I mean," she stammered, face red. "I was told you are engaged."

He groaned. "What can I say, my dear Mary Ann? I could not live without you. And I met someone who reminded me of you. She had your brown hair and smile. Thinking I could never have you, I ended up getting engaged to her."

"But I couldn't do that to her," he continued. "It wasn't fair to her. Or to me. It's you I want Mary Ann. I'm sorry I ever left."

He gripped her hands even tighter. "I won't take 'no' for an answer," he said, his moustache twitching. "I quit my job. If you want to stay here and take care of Mrs. Howard you can. We can live in West Bridgewater and you can come over during the day to be with her. For all I care, we can even live in the old butcher shop in the back of this house. As long as I'm with you I don't care."

Mary Ann was speechless. How could she tell him she thought her life was over when he left? She nodded and said nothing.

He reached out and pulled her close to him. She put her face on his shoulder, ignoring the cold wet snow.

"Excuse me?"

She turned to see Mrs. Howard standing in the doorway, eyebrows arched. Mary Ann slipped her right arm through Horace's and turned to face her benefactor.

"Mrs. Howard," she said, shoulders squared, "I would like you to meet my fiancé."

More Than A Home

The new year began with sunlight glistening on the snow. Icicles sparkled as they dangled from branches. Even old fences looked like artistic masterpieces in the dazzling winter day.

"A new year and a new life" thought Mary Ann, looking out the window from her old room. She trembled with excitement. "And for the very first time, my own home."

January 1, 1885 was a perfect day for her wedding. Mrs. Howard had grudgingly conceded that marriage was a reasonable option for her consort. Garaphilia and Amanda were delighted and showered the young couple with praise.

A simple ceremony was planned at the home of Horace's family. Small and simple is what Mary Ann desired. The bridal gown was a plain white dress. But with the jewelry and sash contributed by Garaphilia, it was elegant.

Horace found a house for rent nearby. It was small, but Mary Ann was overjoyed with it. He laughed at her as he watched her hang the curtains two days after their wedding.

"Oh, Horace. Don't you just love having our own home together?"

"Certainly," he answered. "Much fancier than the blacksmith shop, I must say." His walrus mustache twitched with humor.

"It's wonderful," she sighed. "I can put things where I want

179

them. I can make my own home instead of just keeping some-one else's."

"Well, to be honest," her husband interjected, "I was al-most expecting your darling Mrs. Howard was going to insist you continue to live at her house."

"Horace, you don't know how much it means to me that you were willing to move so close to her. I know Mrs. Howard seems a bit harsh at times, but truly my life would have been so very bad if it wasn't for her. I really must see her through."

"It's who you are," he stated simply.

"And I didn't even know that I could ever be this happy," she answered.

***

The sun tried to break through the clouds on that chill morning. Mists that had covered the land earlier had rolled away, leaving the sun and clouds to compete with each other.

Side by side, Mary Ann and Horace walked out of the church with others at the funeral. They walked the short dis-tance to the cemetery where Mrs. Howard would be buried.

Mary Ann felt numb inside. The weather matched her mood; neither gloomy nor cheerful. She had stayed by the old lady's side to the end; had faithfully attended her after her stroke. She could be satisfied that she had done all that was in her power to keep her comfortable.

Impatiently, she brushed away a nagging fly. She wasn't grief stricken, nor was she at complete peace. "What haunting thought still follows me?" she wondered.

After words were spoken at the grave-site, the mourners began to disperse. Mary Ann lingered. She placed the flowers on Mrs. Howard's grave. She glanced at Mr. Howard's grave to her side. "If it wasn't for them…" she thought once more.

She looked over at her husband. "And where would I go now if Horace had not married me?" She knew no other life. Her savings were meager. "I don't even know how I would go about getting another job," she reflected.

Garaphilia turned toward her. "Mary, how can we ever, ever thank you for all you have done? You have been such a godsend to our family. Mother often said she didn't know where she would be if it wasn't for you."

Mary Ann smiled, "And I have often thought much the same. Your parents were there for me when I needed them. I'm glad I was there for them when they needed me."

Amanda joined them. "Perhaps we have all needed you, much more than you ever knew," she stated quietly. "And I believe my mother was fonder of you than her words may have led you to believe."

The three women grinned with mutual understanding at the disposition of the matron they had lost, easing the somber mood between. "Are you driving to the house with Horace or with us?" Amanda asked.

Mary Ann caught her breath. She glanced at her husband, then the sisters. "I'm not, uh, not sure," she stammered.

Garaphilia spoke up. "Of course you are coming to the house for the reading of the will. You have been part of our family for almost 25 years."

There it was again. Was she a member of the family or was she not?

Horace came to her rescue. "I'll be driving her over to the house," he said. "I can finish one of the fences Mary Ann talked me into repairing for your mother," he added.

Within the hour Mary Ann joined the others in the famil-iar living room. Henry was there, as were Amanda and Garaphilia with their husbands. She sat down in the wooden chair by the window. It had always been her chair.

The lawyer looked around at the group. The room was silent as the seal was broken and the only sound was that of paper unfolding. He cleared his throat and began to read.

It was short. Her estate was to be divided among the three living children.

That was it. Mary Ann was not even mentioned.

She sat stiffly. Amanda and Garaphilia glanced at her, then each other.

"The house and farm will be sold," Henry spoke up. "That money will also be divided between the three of us." The sisters nodded quietly.

"There must be a mistake," Mary Ann thought. "This must be an old will; one that was written before I joined the family." But no, the will had been written since Mr. Howard's death and the death of Sarah, their other daughter.

Back at their own house, Horace bristled with anger.

"That old woman," he almost shouted. "Two dollars a week for the rest of your life and she doesn't even put you in her will! Then again, why should I even be surprised? She would have had you stay with her until you were a fifty year old maid had she lived that long." His whiskers trembled as he spoke.

Mary Ann closed her eyes. "I don't even know what to say. What to think," she stated flatly.

"Oh, believe me, I can think of things to say," he retorted. "Plenty of things. I just wish the old dame was here to hear them."

"Don't Horace. Please, don't," Mary Ann's voice quivered. "I'll find another situation as a house keeper somewhere else and earn some more money, somehow."

He held her in his arms and ran his fingers through her

hair. "It's not the money, I'm upset about. It's you. I always felt you were taken advantage of, in spite of your protests. There's just no denying it."

"But I will try to get another job, Horace."

"No, I don't want you to. You just said you loved keeping your own home instead of someone else's."

***

"My own kitchen," Mary Ann murmured as she added chopped celery to the clam chowder simmering on the stove. She dashed extra pepper into the pot. "I do like the extra pepper, even though Mrs. Howard never did."

She heard Horace coming. He inhaled deeply as the fragrance of homemade bread met him as he opened the door.

"Hmmm, my favorite foods he declared," as he eyed the apple crisp on the counter.

He got cleaned up and joined her at the table. Mary Ann knew something was brewing in his mind. She waited for him to speak.

"I did have a talk with my boss today. He knew a little about the Howards."

"Oh?"

"Told him about the number of years you stayed on with the family. Working for next to nothing and expected to stay with them all the time. Barely allowed to go out and have a cup of coffee on your own time."

"You have mentioned that to me a time or two Horace. Do you really need to discuss your disapproval with the rest of the town?"

"He told me something I think you really ought to hear."

"What is it?"

"He said you should sue the estate. Now, now, don't get so flustered. Hear me out."

"Horace! I could never!"

"Just listen. You don't have to do it if you don't want, but at least you ought to know your rights before you go deciding you won't exercise them."

"You just don't go around suing people who took you in off the street."

"That's it Mary Ann. If you were family, then you should be given an inheritance. If you were a servant, you should be given adequate pay for your years of service. Even servants are given some sort of severance when their employers die or take leave of them."

She stared at him, spoon in midair. "I can't believe you would even ask me to do such a thing."

"I'm not asking you. And I'm certainly not going to tell you to. But, as I've said, my boss has some legal connections. He said you ought to talk to his brother-in-law who's a lawyer. Like I said, they know the family and they know the law about these things."

"And I know my own heart, Horace. I could never, ever sue the family. Why, they are all the family I've got."

He took another sip of his soup. "Some family," he muttered.

The next day Mary Ann was working in the garden. Horace was gone. Married or single, hunting, fishing, and trapping were sports he would not live without. But Mary Ann found them all distasteful. Though Mr. Howard had been a successful custom butcher, she never did like to see the animals killed. Working in her own vegetable garden suited her much better.

Her eyes kept trailing to the open land to the right of her cottage. It was a sunny spot. "The perfect place for a house,"

Mary Ann often thought as she eyed the land. It was well situated. A large vegetable garden, a flower garden, a summer kitchen: Mary Ann could see the landscape in her mind.

The sound of a carriage from the other direction caught her attention. She turned to see Garaphilia dismounting. She removed her gloves and apron.

"Garaphilia! What a pleasant surprise. Please come in."

"Thank you, Mary Ann. I would like to have a word with you."

Garaphilia was seated in the living room as Mary Ann poured tea for them. She was conscience of her small cottage. A colonel's wife, Garaphilia was accustomed to much grander décor.

"Your home is lovely, my dear. And I'm so glad to see your stitchery hanging there."

"Well, it is a rather plain and small house. But I do enjoy fixing it up."

"I'm sure you do," Garaphilia answered. "And that's why I have come over. My sister and I are both appalled that my mother did not have you in her will. That was quite unexpected to me, I must assure you."

She sighed again. "My brother, unfortunately, doesn't necessarily see things in the same light."

Mary Ann bit her lip and looked down at her hands.

Garaphilia continued. "I've talked it over with my husband. We are both of the same mind on this. With all the years of devoted housekeeping and cooking, not to mention companionship, we just can't see you walk away empty handed."

She opened her purse and pulled a paper from it. She reached across and handed it to Mary Ann. "This is for you. You must take it."

Mary Ann reached out her hand and took the check. Her

eyes glanced at it. "Two thousand dollars" was printed in Garaphilia's dainty handwriting.

"Thank you," Mary Ann stated quietly.

"You deserve it," Garaphilia said plainly. "Now I must be leaving. But I wanted to give you the check myself. And," she added, "to let you know that your dedication to my parents was not unnoticed."

Mary Ann walked her to her carriage. She waved as it pulled away.

"I'm so glad I didn't let anyone talk me into suing the family," she thought.

***

Horace came home triumphant. "You just have to see these geese I brought," he announced as she opened the back door. "Aren't they handsome?" Mary Ann wrinkled her nose.

"Well, you have to admit I've had a productive hunt."

"I'm not arguing with your success," she replied.

He stomped his boots at the door. "Then just why are you smirking like that?"

"Horace, so much has happened. I need to tell you."

"Tell me what?" he asked, washing his hands at her sink.

She handed him the check. He glanced down at it, then looked up at her. He looked at the check again.

"Two thousand dollars!"

"Isn't Garaphilia wonderful? And aren't you glad I didn't sue the estate. Think of how terrible I would feel now. Really, their daughters have always treated me so well."

"I'm glad they did. But you never deserved any less."

"Life can be so hard, and we should be thankful for every good thing that comes our way," she answered. "I'm glad the

Howards provided for me as a child, and their daughters have done so now. Do you know what we can do with this money?"

"Well, it's your money for sure. Your inheritance you've every right to. I'm assuming you will want to buy a home instead of renting this cottage."

"Not just buy a home, Horace. I'd love to build our own home. Make it just the way we want it."

"You've had your eyes on the land next door," he prompted. "It's a good piece of land, and I understand the owner would be willing to sale."

She clapped her hands. "I'm so happy, Horace. It will be the perfect house. And Amanda is going to give us some furniture and things. We talked about it."

"Those two sisters have already given us the furnishings we are using in this house. We can move the furniture over, you know."

"But Amanda is also going to give us a cradle and high chair. She has baby furniture she is not using any more."

Her husband's eyes widened. "Baby furniture?"

Her smile lit up her face. "Isn't it wonderful? It's all so perfect."

***

The months flew by. They were able to buy the desired land for a few hundred dollars. And Horace started to build the house. He worked his trade during the day, and came home at night to build their home. Board by board, the house started to take shape.

If he was tired, he didn't show it. He fretted that the house should be ready by the time the baby would come. But that was not possible, and she insisted she didn't mind.

Garaphilia and Amanda and their husbands came over to

see the house in progress. They had suggestions that proved helpful. And true to their word, a bountiful layette appeared for the baby.

The baby came on a warm, sunny day on July 27, 1887. Horace paced back and forth, neither his carpentry nor blacksmith skills of any use. He tried to stay busy. But soon enough he was summoned back to his own cottage. Mary Ann was sitting in bed, holding a bundle.

"It's a girl. A beautiful girl."

He sat by her side on the bed. "She is beautiful. I bet she will have your curls."

"And my glasses?" Mary Ann quipped. They both laughed, and looked again at their daughter.

"I thought it was going to be a girl," her husband stated. "In fact, I was quite sure of it."

"Oh were you now?"

"Yes, and I can even prove it. I'll be right back."

Mary Ann's questioning eyes followed his quick disappearance. Soon he returned and handed her a small box.

"Go ahead," he urged. "Open it."

Curious, Mary Ann removed the paper on the outside. Inside was a porcelain baby with curls. She looked up at him, his face wreathed in smiles.

"See," he declared, "when I saw this baby in the store I just knew you would have a baby girl with your curls. So I bought it. I think it looks just like her, don't you?"

"Yes it does," Mary Ann answered, tracing the curls that framed the delicate face. "This will always have the place of honor in our home."

She placed the porcelain on the night stand and lightly stroked the forehead of the baby in her arms. "Thank you ,Horace. Thank you for the gift. And for building our home.

But there's something so much more important we need to give her."

"Which is?"

Mary Ann looked at him soberly. "I don't want her ever to be alone in the world, like I was," her voice quivered. "I don't want her to have to depend on others and never be confident she can take care of herself."

Horace held her hand and pressed it in agreement.

"The Howards gave me a home," she continued, "And I appreciate it. Deeply. But Mary Emily will have more. My little girl will get an education. I will insist. No one will ever be able to take her independence away from her."

Part 6

Cloudy Skies

Changed Overnight

1948

"Mary Emily," Donna whispered looking intently at the figurine sitting on the shelf and then glancing toward the kitchen where her step-grandmother was now cooking. She had always called her Kithy, just as everyone else did.

But her real name was Mary Emily Atwell Keith. Her father had given the figurine as a gift to her mother when she was born. And her mother had emphasized the need for a woman to make her way in the world, no matter what her circumstances.

Having finished her dusting, Donna replaced the figurine and climbed the steps of their Cape Cod style home. She made her way down the long hallway at the top of the stairs to her room and closed the door behind her. She rummaged through a drawer to find a note-card Marion had given her several months before. On the front was a picture of the cottage where Kithy had been born.

Donna found similarities in her situation and in Kithy's mother. Both longed for their own home, but found others deciding where they would live. "At least I was never auctioned off," Donna reasoned.

She shook her head. "What a contradiction," she thought, as she looked at the picture and pondered Kithy's story. Perhaps Kithy's domineering presence and her thirst for knowledge were planted by her mother who was deprived of both education and control. Kithy, herself, was such a contrast to Donna's Grandmother Hogue in Kansas, the loving woman who planted flowers to spell out her name and who held firmly to a faith that caused her ancestors to cross oceans and traverse continents.

And then there was Florence, the grandmother who gave birth to a baby she gave up for adoption before disappearing forever from their lives. Three very different women they were, these grandmothers whose paths had never crossed, but whose children had woven a net between them. A net, Donna thought with a sigh, that now ensnared her.

Donna sat on her bed tucked into the alcove of the dormer window overlooking the front of the house and surveyed her spacious bedroom. The room was attractively arranged with the maple furniture that her father had bought for her in Boston. Two twin beds were covered with matching white hobnail bedspreads. A black and white photograph of two children sat on the bureau; a picture of Bill holding a ball and she holding her doll taken several years before Dick was born, the only reminder in the room of her life before coming to Massachusetts. The dressing table had a sheer white over-skirt covering a yellow underskirt that highlighted the cheerful yellow rug in the center of the room. "Certainly many others have it much worse," she reflected as her fingers traced the yellow ribbons and white gardenias embossed on the blue wallpaper.

"Perhaps it is better here," she contemplated, as she remembered her mother's crowded apartment and Aunt Cora's farmhouse without electricity. And of course she was spared the farm chores she recalled as she pictured her aunts and uncles and grandparents going about their lives.

Her reverie was interrupted by a knock on her bedroom door. Marion poked her head in. "Janie called for you a few days ago," Marion informed her. "I had invited her to go with us to town tomorrow."

Donna's eyes lit up at the opportunity of seeing her best friend. In Kansas she had moved too frequently to make close friends.

"That would be great," Donna agreed.

Next day the mid-morning sun saw the two teenagers walking in the small downtown area of East Bridgewater heading toward the ice cream parlor. Marion had dropped the two friends off as she made her daily run to the post-office in town.

"So," Janie asked after Donna had described the results of her last week with her mother, "Do you wish you had stayed in Kansas, or would you rather be here?"

"That's the thing," Donna responded. "I love both my parents, but neither of them seems to care much where I go. On the other hand, Marion and Kithy want me here; and I know Aunt Cora wants me too."

"Well, I guess that means you belong to all of us," said Janie, slipping her arm through Donna's. "And I have to say I would have been devastated if you didn't come back. Don't you want to go to high school with the rest of us?"

High school. In only a few short weeks they would be starting together at the big school. It gave the girls plenty to talk about. The rest of the morning was spent planning wardrobes and discussing after school activities and Donna quickly forgot her nagging misgivings.

But that night, news from Kansas reminded her again.

"I got a letter from my mother," her father announced at the table. The family was seated at the long mahogany table in the dining room. Her father was seated at one end of the table and Kithy at the other end. Donna took her eyes off the china pattern she had been inspecting to turn to the envelope in her father's hand. "Seems my brother Bob will be coming out with his wife Margaret in a few weeks."

"Uncle Bob and Aunt Margaret!" Donna exclaimed. "Coming here?" She looked over at Bill who seemed as surprised as she.

Through the rest of the meal, Donna described her aunt and uncle to her stepmother and grandmother. She told them how Uncle Bob lived diagonally across from Grandma and Grandpa Hogue's farm. Bill added information about Aunt Margaret as Kithy and Marion plied them with questions.

When she finished eating Marion headed to the kitchen and began filling the sink with soapy water. Her husband unexpectedly followed her. The murmur of their low voices reached the dining room.

Donna carried her dishes from the table to the kitchen. "We're talking now," her father's voice was gruff. "You can bring the dishes in later." Marion looked at her without speaking. She did not look pleased, whatever they were discussing.

Donna headed back to the dining room where Kithy looked at her with raised eyebrows. She shrugged her shoulders at her grandmother and brother. "What else was in the letter from Grandma Hogue?" she wondered silently.

Whatever it was, it seemed to have decreased Marion's enthusiasm for entertaining company from the Midwest. She asked no more questions about her brother-in-law and sister-in-law. But then again, school was starting for her in a few weeks, and she had plenty to keep her busy getting ready for a new class of third grade pupils.

Donna was also occupied. Daily she and Janie met face to face or talked over the phone about school. She eagerly anticipated showing Uncle Bob and Aunt Margaret her home on the East Coast, her first opportunity to be the hostess for any of her Kansas relatives. Enthusiastically, she helped Marion take down curtains to clean and get the guest room ready.

Donna rode with Marion and her father to South Station in Boston to meet her aunt and uncle. She spotted Margaret as she exited the train and waved excitedly to her aunt. Then she stopped abruptly. Emerging from the train was her uncle and a small boy. She looked again. There was no question. Her brother Dick was with them. She looked at her father for an explanation, but he gave none. He stepped up to meet his brother and sister-in-law without any sign of surprise.

"Dick?" Donna said, walking up to the little boy. "Dick," she said again as she hugged him. "I didn't know you were coming."

"I came to see you at your house," he said.

"Here you are, Donna," Aunt Margaret stated. "Yes, we brought Dick along with us too."

Donna held his hand as they walked to the car. She sat next to him on the forty-five minute trip back to the town of East Bridgewater.

The next few days were busy for the household. Marion took Aunt Margaret shopping. Sometimes Donna accompanied them. She tagged along as her uncle inspected different buildings her father had constructed. Donna particularly liked taking her relatives to the family's favorite restaurants.

The third day after their arrival Marion and Howard announced they were taking Uncle Bob and Aunt Margaret out to eat alone. Bill informed them that he had a date that evening. At Marion's suggestion, Donna called Janie and invited her to go to the afternoon matinee. The two girls took Dick with them to watch the movie.

Coming out of the movie theatre, they saw Marion's car waiting for them. But it was not Marion behind the wheel.

"Hi, Bill. This is a surprise," his sister said as the trio climbed into the car. "I thought you were going on a date."

"Change of plans," he answered briefly.

"Well, you should have come to the movies with us," she continued as the car pulled away. Bill did not answer and the two girls looked at each other and shrugged. He dropped Janie off at her house, and then headed toward home.

"You know what, Bill? This is the first time all three of us have been in the same car in seven years."

"Yep" he answered quietly.

"And it's the first time in our lives the three of us were alone together," she noted.

Bill just shook his head as the car pulled into the driveway. He looked sadly at his sister. "It may be a while before it happens again," he stated quietly. He pocketed the keys and headed toward the front door.

"What's wrong, Bill?" his sister asked following him. "Aren't you going out tonight?

"Nope."

"Why not? Did she not want to go out with you after all?"

"No, Sis it's not that. Seemed to me tonight would be a good time to stay home." He nodded toward the front door. Curious, Donna walked up the steps. She noticed her father's car in the driveway. The adults were already back.

"How was the movie?" Marion asked cheerfully as they entered. Dick went upstairs as Bill and Donna headed into the living room. Her father, stepmother, and Kithy were sitting there, apparently waiting for them.

"Where are Aunt Margaret and Uncle Bob?" Donna asked.

"They left," her father replied.

"Left?"

"Yes," Marion answered, "they are on the train to Kansas."

"Left to go back to Kansas? Already?" Donna asked incredulously.

"Yes, they are on their way back now," her father stated.

"So soon? Without Dick?"

"That's right. We thought it would be easier this way," he informed her.

"Do you mean," Donna asked, "that all this time all of you knew they were going to bring Dick here and leave him?"

"That was the idea," her father answered.

"And did anyone tell Dick that?"

No one spoke. She heard Bill shuffling uneasily behind her.

"Look Donna," her father said. "My mother has been taking care of Dick since he was a baby. I got a letter from her saying that since I was now married and you were living with me, it was time for me to take Dick as well."

"This was Grandma Hogue's idea?" Donna was stunned.

"She felt she was getting too old to raise a small child and that the boy belonged in a family with a mother and father."

Donna turned toward her brother. "Did you know about this?"

He shook his head. "No," he answered. "Not until after you left today to go to the movies."

"But why?" Donna turned back to the three adults sitting in the room. "Bill lives with Grandma and Grandpa. He has for years. Why can't Bill and Dick stay together?"

"Bill's in high school. He refuses to stay in Massachusetts. But Dick is young enough he will do as I say," her father answered.

"And did anyone ask Dick what he wanted?"

Her father's eyes narrowed. His voice was cold. "It isn't the child's right to decide where he is going to live."

"But the farm was his home. He didn't even have a chance to say good-bye. You can't just change everything overnight on him!" Donna had never talked back to her father before.

"That's enough," her father's voice was raised. "My brother is gone and Dick will not be going back to Kansas. It's final."

Behind her a small sob was heard. Donna pivoted to find Dick standing behind her.

"I want to go home," he pleaded. "I want Grandma."

The room was silent. The boy's lip quivered.

"It's time for both of you to go upstairs," her father barked.

Donna reached for her brother's small hand. At the foot of the stairs she turned and glared at the adults staring at each other in the living room. Hand in hand they walked up the stairs together and into the middle bedroom where Dick slept.

"I want Grandma and Grandpa," he said again as his tears fell.

"It's okay Dick," his sister tried to soothe him. "I missed everyone when I came back here too. I did at first. But I like it here now."

"I want to go home. I want my toys and my bed," he whimpered.

"I know, Dick. I know," she crooned. "But you know what? You're like me now. You have two homes – one here and one in Kansas. Not everyone has that. We get to travel and see people when we have two homes."

"I want to stay with Grandpa and Grandma. I want to work on the farm with Bill."

"That's the hardest part," his sister agreed. She tried to keep her voice from shaking. "I miss Bill a lot too," she whispered. No one ever knew, she reflected. In all the years no one had ever asked about the pain she suffered separated from her older brother. For the first time in her life there was someone else who understood, and she wanted to spare him.

She rubbed the back of the weeping child until his sobs subsided. After a while his regular breathing let her know he had fallen asleep.

Slowly she dragged herself to her own bedroom and closed the door.

"It's not fair," she declared to the furniture. "How dare they treat him like...like..." Her eyes darted around the room. She caught a glimpse of her own reflection on the bureau mirror. Beneath was the picture of herself and Bill as children before her parents separated.

"Like they treated me," she whispered.

On These Shores

Sunlight struggled to break through the clouded skies when Donna awoke the next morning. She was lying on her bed, still in her clothes. It was the last day of summer vacation before the new school year began.

She sighed as she remembered her little brother. He had planned to go to school in several weeks in Kansas with his kindergarten friends. Overnight, his whole world had changed.

Light steps in the hallway were treading toward her room. Marion's staccato rap was heard on the door. Donna did not turn her face from the wall as she heard the bedroom door open.

"Good morning," her stepmother's voice sang, cheerful even if a bit unnatural. "Kithy suggested a trip to the beach today. It's our last day before school."

Donna was stunned that her stepmother would think of going to the beach. But on second thought, perhaps it would bring comfort to her brother.

"Lunch at Bert's" Marion called out. "Better get yourself dressed and have some breakfast now."

It took little time for Donna to change. She saw Kithy gathering items for their day trip. Her father had left, and Bill had gone with him. In spite of Kithy's plan to include Bill on their lunch at Bert's, he had declined the invitation and left with his father an hour earlier. Donna found Dick in the kitchen at the breakfast table. She saw his white face and red eyes. Apparently his night had been worse than hers.

Marion drove her black Plymouth. Donna and Dick sat in the back seat. She looked vacantly out the window as the scenery passed. He stared straight ahead. The two women sitting up front chatted.

"I could use some shells and star fish for my third grade class," Marion hinted. "We will be studying the ocean next month."

"You can get your own sea shells," Donna wanted to retort. Instead she bit her lip and said nothing.

The thirty minute trip to the Atlantic Ocean took them to the town of Plymouth and the beach by Bert's Diner. Donna left the car and strode down the beach as Marion and Kithy put up a beach umbrella at the location Kithy indicated. Dick was on his knees feeling the unfamiliar texture of the sand run through his fingers.

The thundering waves and splashing mists accosted Donna as she walked. A hundred yards away, she turned her back on the others and wandered knee deep into the churning, salty water. The wet sand slipped between her toes and the cold, salt spray splashed across her face. She stared across the vast, unending ocean whose waves were rushing toward her.

It was to this very shore that her ancestors had come. They had come seeking freedom and a new life. Wave upon wave had crossed this ocean and landed up and down this coast. And from here they had spread across the continent to the western shore. Escaping the old world, they forged a new one.

"And they sure made a shambles of it too," Donna reflected, angrily kicking away sea weed that swirled around her ankles. "All the grandiose talk of life, liberty, and the pursuit of happiness and they can't even take care of their own kids."

"All those years," Donna thought, "they moved me from home to home. And now they do it to Dick. Why? Why?"

She struck out at the water once again.

"And then my mother!" Her fists clenched as she remembered. "Dad won't let me live with her and she doesn't want me to. Then I come back here and I can't even talk about her."

What was it Aunt Pearl had said to her? "It's hardest to forgive those who don't even bother to know they've done you wrong." Nobody seemed to care enough about her and her brothers to notice how their actions affected them. Sometimes it felt like all of them had conspired against her.

All of them but Cora, Donna thought. Aunt Cora: the gentle woman who had raised three generations of children who were not her own. The world was a much better place because of people like her.

And Uncle Evert. She had missed him when they wouldn't let her see him again after he wanted to adopt her. She could write to the others; she couldn't even write to him.

She thought of Grandma and Grandpa Hogue. How much she and her brothers loved the farm and the animals and the grandparents who managed it all. She was glad all her moves included time with them. Memories of aunts and uncles in Kansas swept over her thoughts even as the ocean waves swept her legs. Perhaps an Unseen Presence had been with her after all, bringing people to care for her when she was unable to care for herself.

And Marion and Kithy too. She was aware of them sitting on the beach watching her. They weren't sure what to think of all her Midwestern relatives, but they had opened their hearts to her. In return, they found themselves in custody of a small boy they hadn't asked for. What, after all, did they really owe her or Dick anyway?

All these crazy, annoying, but beautiful people who struggled with each other but had tried to make a better world for her when her own had come tumbling down. Isn't that what each generation before had done? The very reason the pilgrims and pioneers had sought these shores? Like her, they all had pain they wanted to put behind and dreams of a golden future that propelled them forward. Maybe they also found that things didn't turn out as they planned; that their own cities of gold weren't sitting here waiting for them. Maybe happiness takes more than being in a different place or with certain people.

"You can be bitter, or you can forgive." She could almost hear Aunt Pearl's voice.

What about her parents? Their refusal to work things out caused all this mess. Was she expected to forgive them too?

Yes, her parents had been selfish at times. But come to think of it, so had she. Hadn't she gone out to Kansas to get her relatives to agree with her plan? Were her intentions really any better than theirs?

"I can't swim."

Donna turned to the small voice behind her. Dick had silently followed her and was standing behind her on the sand grasping the handle of his pail. His sad, innocent blue eyes looked into hers.

"Now it's my turn," Donna thought. "Should I pass my bitterness to this child?" She walked the few feet to where he stood watching her.

"I can't swim either, Dick," Donna replied, kneeling down eye to eye with her brother. "I've always loved the beach but hated swimming. But I tell you what. Let's fill your bucket with shells for Marion's classroom. Do you want to?"

Dick's spontaneous smile answered her question.

"Okay. And we'll get extra so Bill can take them back to Kansas for Mother."

"Can we get some for Grandma Hogue too?"

"Yes, we can get some for Grandma and Grandpa, and Aunt Verna, and Aunt Cora, and Uncle Nathan, and Aunt Pearl. Then all of the people in our home in Kansas will have a present from us from our home in Massachusetts. Would you like that?"

His head nodded enthusiastically. Then he stopped, and a shadow came across his face. "Donna, if we pick up all the shells will there be any left?"

"Don't worry, Dick," Donna laughed, "we won't ever run out of shells. The ocean is filled with clams whose shells wash up to shore and get crushed into sand by the waves. We'll never run out of shells or sand." Donna straightened up and pointed across the horizon.

"See, it's a big, big ocean. In fact, while we pick the shells, I'll tell you the story of the ships that crossed the sea from far way. You know why they sailed here? They left their big cities and their schools and homes and everything they knew and came to build a new home here."

The little boy stood clutching his pail and looking up at her with big eyes. She reached for his hand and he took it trustingly.

"Instead of being angry at the old world," Donna told him, "they wanted to start a new life, find new friends, and make the world a better place. Otherwise, you only get angry and bitter."

"You know, Dick," his sister continued, "You can't change the whole world. But instead of getting mad, you can forgive and try to make it a better place for just one more person." She felt his small hand squeeze hers and saw his head nod as

206

he listened to her words.

Side by side, brother and sister walked down the beach together.

Family Tree

Siblings are listed in boxes with the direct ancestor's name in bold print. For space most siblings are not listed unless mentiond.

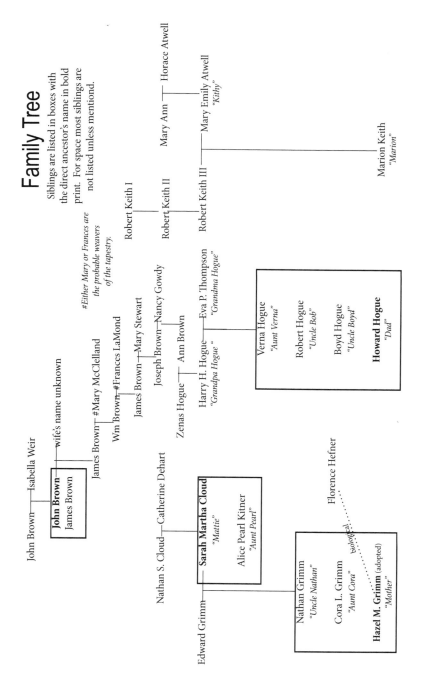

John Brown — Isabella Weir

John Brown
James Brown

— wife's name unknown

James Brown — #Mary McClelland

#Either Mary or Frances are the probable weavers of the tapestry.

Wm Brown — #Frances LaMond

James Brown — Mary Stewart

Joseph Brown — Nancy Gowdy

Ann Brown

Zenas Hogue — Ann Brown

Harry H. Hogue — Eva P. Thompson
"Grandpa Hogue" *"Grandma Hogue"*

Robert Keith I

Robert Keith II

Robert Keith III

Mary Ann — Horace Atwell

Mary Emily Atwell
"Kithy"

Marion Keith
"Marion"

Verna Hogue
"Aunt Verna"

Robert Hogue
"Uncle Bob"

Boyd Hogue
"Uncle Boyd"

Howard Hogue
"Dad"

Nathan S. Cloud — Catherine Dehart

Sarah Martha Cloud
"Mattie"

Alice Pearl Kitner
"Aunt Pearl"

Florence Hefner

Edward Grimm

Nathan Grimm
"Uncle Nathan"

Cora L. Grimm
"Aunt Cora"

biological

Hazel M. Grimm (adopted)
"Mother"

Made in the USA
Middletown, DE
30 April 2015